The Universe,
and Other Fictions

By Paul West

Sheer Fiction
(essays)

Rat Man of Paris
Out of My Depths: A Swimmer in the Universe
(nonfiction)
The Very Rich Hours of Count von Stauffenberg
Gala
Words for a Deaf Daughter (memoir)
Caliban's Filibuster
Colonel Mint
Bela Lugosi's White Christmas
I'm Expecting to Live Quite Soon
Alley Jaggers
Tenement of Clay
I, Said the Sparrow (memoir)
The Snow Leopard (poetry)
The Wine of Absurdity (essays)
Byron and the Spoiler's Art (criticism)

The Universe, and Other Fictions

Short Fiction
by
Paul West

The Overlook Press
Woodstock, New York

First published in 1988 by
The Overlook Press
Lewis Hollow Road
Woodstock, New York 12498

Library of Congress Cataloging-in-Publication Data
West, Paul, 1930-   The universe, and other fictions.
I. Title.
PR6073.E766U5   1988   813'.54   87-42889
ISBN: 0-87951-303-9 (cloth)
ISBN: 0-87951-316-0 (paper)

Some of these stories previously appeared, in sometimes different form, in the following: *Conjunctions, The Cornell Review, Denver Quarterly, Modern Occasions, Mother Jones, New American Review, The American Pen, The Paris Review, Partisan Review, Remington Review, The New Directions International Literary Anthologies, Sites*, and, in translation, in *Quimera* (Barcelona) and *SyNTAXIS* (Tenerife).

CONTENTS

Contents

1.
Life with Atlas

I no sooner thought than I began to withdraw from the consequences; understand, if you will, the embarrassments of being a vicarious voice: I, hearing Atlas, uttered him, but in no way managing to reproduce the intonations, nuances, or even the tart symphonic thrust of the voice I heard. And now, thanks be Fortune, Atlas is coming out as words, and I'm in the near-fatuous position of transposing a voice-in-the-head, but spoken into the tape by myself, into yet another medium, of which not even my best friend, Etna, would call me master. What is indisputably missing is the electric thrill of his very presence, a kind of massive vibrancy that makes you feel you've been plugged, for the first time, into the source of things. So it was much more than a voice I communicated with, for me at any rate; it was the Atlas of that Fourth-Century B.C. vase painting, in which he appears as a light-limbed boxer holding up both arms in a victory salute, except that resting on his palms there is a lightweight-looking flying saucer, maybe of aluminum, while to his left there prances a magical horse near some bushes, to his right there stands somebody giving him the two-finger sign, to which Atlas attends by looking sideways and a bit downward. I know this is a feeble account of the picture, doing scant justice to his trim insouciance, but it will have to serve. After all, I didn't ask him to come to me; there are thousands he'd have fared better with, but perhaps my being a former world traveler who has settled down, priding myself on my ability to stay put, had something to do with it. In common we have the static, not to mention an overview of the world, and a developed sense of being excluded: he from liberty (or even rest or leave), I from Peking.

Clearly, anyone determined to object will accuse me of imagining the whole thing; let him pass in peace and go on to read about the Decline and Fall of the Roman Empire. I faced that objection from the outset, knowing that from time to time I would catch myself half-supplying Atlas with Atlasisms; but then, a good listener always psychs and second-guesses, and even UN translators have been known to come up with prophetic renderings: three or four words of translation before the original is uttered. Such poachings or previsions are part of cranial voxology, take my word for it. Just as I went on taking Atlas's own. When the Voice of the Ages (or whatever) deigns to favor you with some friendly gab, you don't make picayune cracks about the quality of reception, the speed or slowness of the transmission, the timbre of his vowels, and you certainly don't mind that occasionally you get lost in him, he in you, the pair of you in the maze of triply-transposed transcription. Man can always, if he weakens, go ape, whereas ape can never go man; I sometimes tell myself that when especially lamenting some gross piece of international mayhem. It soothes me somewhat; it's half-true; and it's five seconds killed. Just think how Atlas had to kill time, always at his station, never resting, always under the circumstances, never without an ache; no wonder he learned how to make the mind go blank.

Blank brought me back to the crisis in hand. Tempted to breach civility and counsel Atlas to get off the pot, I ferreted around in my own head for some way of helping him either to adjust or to strike clear and away. Mentally ready to shift, he was too far gone for the physical part, meaning he could always imagine himself out of anything; the eons of stoical duty had groomed him too well. Was I right in encouraging him to stay where, and as, he was? Was that selfish? Not if I made a sacrifice or two myself. What Atlas needed wasn't an initiative, but company, and so long as his voice kept on coming I'd be more than glad to partner him. Therefore, keep it coming by the gift of company nonstop! Invite him in, not only into my head, but into my life. Have him, somehow, meet Frank Etna, landlord extraordinary; share in the stapling of the daily-longer sherry-sack cape; fill him in on food and the pleasures of the American bathroom . . . The only one elect, so far as I knew, I was elated; my eyes leaked driblets of joy, my hands quivered with fellow-feeling.

"Are you there?" I asked him. "Any things you want to know? That you don't already. Or things you want done."

There ensued the kind of silence in which you imagine you can hear plants growing.

Heedless of plants, I asked again, prefixing the question with his call letters enlivened into Aardvark, Tabernacle, Labium, Aardvark, Sabbath. And that fetched him back.

Laughing (a sound of heavy chains being twirled in thick oil), he gave an answer I didn't expect: "Why has the Astronomer-Royal quit Greenwich, and its meridian, and moved to Sussex? Why didn't the English epicure stay put, like me? It's disorienting. And disoccidentalizing as well."

I said something about pollution, peace, urban overspill, heard an Atlas-snort followed by another question: "Haven't I seen gold-plated telescopes mounted in Lear jets?" He had indeed; I'd seen that on a TV special. "Better visibility," I guessed.

"You're wondering, I bet, why I'm so goddamned astronomical!"

True, I was.

"Occupational—ur, hazard, buddy-boy. Skip it. Maybe you can tell me the meaning of a phrase I caught the other year: 'World Premiere Encore.' If you ask me, that's contradictory: if it's a premiere, it is; if it's an encore, it's that. It sure as Atlas ain't both."

I apologized for the golden tongues of Madison Avenue, drawing his attention to fool's gold, muck and brass, and the overall deterioration of the language, and the disappearance of the verb, the plague of the abstract noun and the emasculated verb, the verb *to be*.

"By the way, Thor," I heard next, "there was no Big Bang. Had there been one, I'd have known. It's always been steady state up here, just the gods that reel now and then. Took me a mite of time to realize it, but I'm the main part of that steadiness. I never had a beginning, I always was, and all that stuff about Pops and Grandad is just a concession to cosmic respectability. I'm an uncaused effect, no doubt the first of the tribe you've ever beat gums with."

Gulping "For sure, for sure," I asked him if he knew about—oh, a random sampling of our daily lives down here—passports, cucumbers, waste disposals, penicillin, fiber-point pens, hi-fi equipment, air conditioning, mouthwash, Scotch tape, scissors, DDT, and Neapolitan ice cream. He knew the lot, seemed vaguely bored with it, and delivered me a counterquota of Atlas-tropes, none of which I understood (not that I was meant to): such things as orb-torque, neutrino-nests, galaxy-starvation, antenna-warp, dustball pool, nova-fishing, sungunnery, nebul-ovens, mirror-zero, Mars-exemption, gamma-slang, and quasar-cosmetics. As well as much more, a quick and humbling sample of the cosmic Sears and Roebuck catalogue.

All I could retaliate with was something else I'd heard on TV, something about the end of the universe: "After thirty thousand million years more," I brashly told him, "the whole thing will come to rest and then begin to contract. Whether the universe will then bounce back is anyone's guess. I won't be here to check the answers."

All I could hear was galactic buzz.

Told him so. Where was he?

Still only the buzz. What is it then?

"We call it interferon," he said haughtily. "Nothing to do with the terrestrial common cold, something—not that anyone in your vicinity'd understand it—to do with argon. You guys don't want to be facetious, else the powers-that-be'll lay three dozen Second Comings on you, all on Fridays, just to fox you. You'd better not smartmouth about the End of anything; we don't deal in ends, we deal in currencies, nothing to do with money either!"

Somehow Atlas was ruder, that was it; confidence gained had sapped his manners, and I was just going to object when

I thought better of it. After all (and when I thought that phrase I really meant it: he *was* After All), who knows how many eons he'd spent trying to get through.

So I just said "Sorry: never being in the know gets us on the raw. We act up verbally when our minds draw blanks."

A change of tack was imperative—it was no use slanging each other with our respective systems—so I begged his permission to quiz him about such of his past as hadn't made the primers in myth. "Did you ever get to college? If you have them there?"

"Pro, he spent three light-years at Panbridge, and Epi about the same time—amount of time—at Luxford. But me, I was a drop-out, took some evening classes in weight-lifting at the Vulcan Institute, but I found even that a bore. I guess I was only anticipating my vocation. Fact is, there was nothing lying around heavy enough for me to practice on, so it's just as well there was a universe handy. Else I'd have been out of commission for keeps. Just imagine what it's like being eternal when there's not a thing you can do."

Quick as a fisherman striking, I asked him, "If that is so, why all the fuss about suicide? No such thing for you. Why, you could walk out from under, and even if it all came tumbling down, you'd be OK. Although where you'd be, I've no idea."

His life, he told me, was his occupation, his worst fear being choreless.

"I prefer world-sadness, world-weariness," he added, "to being unemployed. But it's not all been depressing. Back in the thirties I think it was, my daughter Maia, best known as the mother of Mercury, talked up such a storm in the ether that a team of airplane designers actually designed and built a mother flying-boat named after her, with a smaller but four-engined second flying-boat atop her on a mount, and that was Mercury. Eight engines between them! I dearly loved to watch them lift off the old briny, not so much wine-dark as beer-bright, and then Mercury would lift off from the mother ship at about five thousand feet. And then they played tag all over the airways, Mercury feinting at her hull as if trying to suck on her babylike, and Maia lumbering about a bit being so broad in the beam. He zipped and flitted, she droned and mumbled; he caught more of the light than she, his wings like blades, while she, with much broader wings, seemed like some giant manta-ray cruising ever below him in case he fell."

Did I detect a throb in that rusty voice? I did indeed.

"Proud of your grandson, Atlas?"

"Maia, one of the seven Pleiades, you know, she was the smartest of them all, got herself written up in the glossies as Maia Majestas, Fauna, Bona Dea, Ops, the whole bit. I guess she'd rate as a kind of Sophia Bergman of infolded space. Mercury, though, he'd the smarts beyond compare; it figures, I guess, if you're Maia to begin with and old Zeusy-Boy slips you a foaming schlong's-length, ur—it figures you'd get a prodigy of some kind out of that. He once stole, and hid in a cave, fifty head of cattle; yep, Hermes, as I sometimes call him—Herm or Merc—was one of the first cattle rustlers in pre-history! As they always say about him, born in the a.m., he'd invented the lyre by noon. That's the kind of speed he flew at. Sure, he was a big show-off even as a kid, but who wants a dumbbell for a grandson? Merc was some boy, fast as light, slippery-tongued, impossible to best in an argument; spent a good deal of his time operating as a Western Union galactogram-bearer, though he did hundreds of other things as well—a kind of winged cartel. I sometimes thought he'd taken on too much—agronomy, rhetoric, business management, heraldry, boxing, languages, astronomy, communications, and even funeral-parlor practice, you name it, he did a bit of it, sometimes even a lot. What really poisoned him was the cult they made of him on your own planet, casing up little blobs of him in glass bulbs to tell the temperature by. He liked the functional part, but hated the cooped-up feeling the mercury transmitted back to him. But, boy, when he flew, like a tiny fast moon round his Ma, there was red-shift to beat all, and for days after there was background rainbow fit to beat the band. Where those seaplanes went to, we never found out; maybe mothballed someplace. I guess it was one hell of an impractical idea, having one on the other's back like that, dolphin on the whale, and the fuel consumption was out of sight. But it kind of made the family loom a bit larger than usual in the suburbs, see? Instead of being so shadowy (see the pesky ikons they made of me!), we seemed to be substantially there right in front of folks' eyes, like architecture, except it moved, and when it moved it took off and flew, and when it flew it split in half and when it'd split in half it stole parabolas from the spherical geometry of Zeus himself! but they always had to touch down separately, of course, which kind of spoiled the action. I always wished they'd been able somehow to link up again in flight, but I guess that was asking too much. Say, maybe, some day, you could find out for me about that double-decker airplane, where it's at now, what decided them to junk it. Just the sound of those engines blasting for the Off would remove tons from the load on the top of my head. Try?"

Try? I promised I'd *succeed*, certain I could dig up some-thing somewhere in the library. But why, I mused, didn't he know? Maybe part of his punishment was to feel informed without having the facts. Maybe he knew, after all, but no longer realized that he knew; a fact unused is one of knowl-edge's pariahs. It was no use wondering, Atlas was already into other things, still joyfully commemorating Maia, but more intimate in tone.

"Once in a while, she'd zoom up behind me and give me a neck rub, working all the way from below my shoulder blades up to the base of my skull, kneading and smoothing until the blood began to run again. You've never *ported*, have you? But you sure know what it's like to have a stiff neck, when the cords feel like leather-bound drill sticks. But that wasn't all, no sir! Round front, with daughterly delicacy, she'd nuzzle the bridge of my nose, tweak it and pinch it and sometimes put the balls of her thumbs against the top of the eye-sockets. Talk about relief! You know the kind of ache that builds up around there. And, on special days, she'd even nip the flesh between my eyes with her teeth—I must be the only guy in creation with hickeys in that particular spot. A great one for kissing, she was, my Maia: not just the routine stuff, glancing little smooches on the side of my mouth and the tip of my nose, that goes without saying, but when the mood took her she'd pretend I'd (as she'd say) fifteen thousand secret ears, visible to her alone, and she'd go about kissing each one of them in turn. Of course, she didn't, but that was our fancy. Who was I to protest or be literal? It was the only attention I ever got, therefore the best. To cool me off, she'd blow against my closed eyes—you can't imagine the glare I have to put up with, this near umpteen suns—and then she'd just set her head against the side of my neck and stay that way for long hours, murmuring and cooing. A cool, velvet skin she had, like a tegument made of milk. 'Scuse the fancy way of putting it, there're times I get down-right sentimental about the way things were. She'd even, once a month, clean up my back; I mean squeeze out the black holes, clean out the pores. It was mostly accumulated cosmic dust, I guess. Time was I never knew where my back ended and space began, so I guess it's no miracle I was pitted with tiny craters where shrunken stars of almost incalculable gravity stuck and stayed put, all the time getting smaller and heavier, black to the point of invisibility. It's not everyone who'd take on such chores, but Maia did—at least until she had Mercury. He kept her busy from the first, conned her into being less flighty, I guess. He even persuaded her to stop one habit she had; instead of wearing false eyelashes for a social occasion—a state visit by Zeus, all tuxedo and talc—she used to fasten a couple of hummingbirds to her eyelids, and that gave her eyes an incredible hypnotic flutter. Yes sir, those were the old days! Been none like 'em since." There is a slight sob in his voice; I try to cheer him, cannot; he sighs with enormous resonance.

Then says "The past tense, see."

"How was that?"

Atlas sounds like he's cracking up. "She even used to burp me; all I ever got to sustain me was crab-nebula meat, always too hot, always gritty. No, I didn't mean that. You know about my daughters, don't you?" Without waiting for my response he blurted it right out: "The Pleiades: the seven-set. Maia was one of them, see. For some reason they were all born on a mountainside, which made 'em sometimes walk the wee-est bit gimpy. See, I can't bring myself to say it. Well: they all killed themselves, all committed suicide. To a one. Alcyone, Celaeno, Electra, Taygete, Sterope, Aero (a special one that), and even my own Maia. For why? Because the plight of their Dad upset them so. That's all. They couldn't take it eon after eon of seeing him stuck there with his back stiff as a ramrod, forever on cosmic parade, head held high, the whole caboodle on his back. With no hope of remission, no sabbatical. I've heard other versions: it was the death of their sisters, the Hyades, that broke their hearts, or it was Orion's fault, forever propositioning them, until old fussy Zeus, he said 'Enough of this bull, I'll turn them all into stars, Orion as well.' I don't much go for those two particular explanations. But the long and the short of it is all seven of them are stars, and the only converse a tired old titan can have with them is in mid-May, when they signal the approach of harvest-time by rising—out there in Taurus, in the northern hemisphere—and then again, in October, when they set, and that's the time to sow. To some, I gather, they signal the opening and closing of the sailing season, but who cares? What grieves me, among other things, is that one of them, Aero (sometimes Merope to the gossip columnists) isn't even visible. Got herself into a bad marriage with a slippery customer called Sisyphus, and then he got himself a life sentence rolling a block of stone uphill. No doubt you've heard of him: another of Zeus's punitive measures. Do you wonder she can't bear to show her face? Her Dad and husband both, penal servitude for life. It's enough to make a statue weep. Up here, among all the jamming, I hear radio of all kinds, much of it high-falutin chatter about totalitarianism, so-called. Let me tell you, Thor, old buddy, they invented that condition for Atlas (and a few more such as Sisyphus, whom I call Cissyfuss). Nobody knows what being a prisoner's like until he's had a dose of being Atlas fifty or a hundred years, with not even a chance of your good conduct's being taken into account. And then your daughters kill themselves off, they can't stand it. How do you like *them* apples? Just about as far as you can get from golden ones. I'd give a hell of a lot for just one glimpse of Aero's face, those wide and liquid-gray, quicksilver eyes, the neat light brown widow's peak she had, the nose that wasn't snub and wasn't schnozz either. The rest of the world, if it thinks about them at all, reckons them seven (or six) doves; Pleiades sounds like the Greek for dove, see. But I don't much go for that, I remember them as they were: daughters of the Ocean-nymph Pleione, long gone. Sure I had favorites; I know you shouldn't, if you believe all the bullshit the pediatricians hand you, but I did. That's that. I still do. But it's been mighty quiet up here since their conversion, so-called. Hey, you ever tried, between May and October, to pick out seven (or six) particular stars from the hundreds of 'em in Taurus? It's damn nearly impossible. I know the girls are there, but I'm never certain which is which, or even if I haven't looked at the wrong seven. Sure it hurts; another of Zeus's power-ploys. You'd do well to watch out yourself, parleying with the likes of me. He's not one to take things lying down. Anyhow, as I was saying, I stand here and try to cheer myself up with little reminiscences; Pleiades, I say, they're an open cluster of stars, and the luminescent spikes I see attached to them aren't even there, they're diffraction effects in the eye of the beholder, some cloudy spot on the cornea, otherwise known as nebula.

That kind of consolation's like drinking nitric acid. As stars go, they're young, those Pleiades, whereas those Hyades, they . . ."

The voice dwindled to a chaffering of airwaves, a sound as of light flails, either black-body background radiation or merely Atlas groaning in the hoosegow of his mind. I tried to prompt him back to the Hyades, those other daughters, of whom he'd had nothing to say, only he held off, finally broke into some practiced-sounding patter about pleiotropisms and asterisms, about being not only behind the times but also ahead of them, under and above them: a bout of intergalactic self-pity, as he himself called it. Then by gradual allusion, he returned to the business of the daughters, his voice creaky with loss, I could tell that, and his idiom oddly impersonal, for reasons that seemed obvious. "Know what? I don't even recall the names of the Hyades, I'm not even sure if there were two, or five, or six. Everything about them's mighty vague. Half-sisters of the others. Nurses they were, that's one fact. Also in Taurus, but much older than Maia's bunch. Aethra was their mother. Named, all of them, after the Greek for *rain*. Rain stars, that's what they are, but the goddamned Romans got it wrong and, because the Greek word sounded like their word for pig, called them the little pigs. This little pig went to market, this little pig stayed home: well, it's now known what they did as little pigs. As nurses, they breastfed the infant Dionysus and as a reward were made into stars. Couldn't get my attention any other way, I guess. I suppose I now and then catch sight of them up there in Taurus when I'm looking for the other seven. Being older, the Hyades I mean, they've already achieved white dwarf status, pretty shrunken by now, some of them already black dwarfs I wouldn't doubt and maybe even invisible at that. *You* know how it goes: as they cool down, they radiate less and less, and then, when they're cold and dead, they have colossal density, millions of times that of water, say. They're actually smaller than planet Earth, but their mass is like that of the Sun. Takes billions of years to get 'em to that point, of course, but get there they have gotten. They're kind of just memories, I guess, maybe not even that. Whereas Maia and Aero, well . . ."

Again silence found him and lost him, as it sometimes did Frank Etna, my almost-forgotten friend, on his return from yet another raid on the world's wonders: exuberantly recalling how it was to have gone lundy-fishing in Iceland, catching birds on a cliff with a net, or playing aqua-lung cowboy with the tunny deep off Gibraltar, he'd suddenly seize up, look into the middle distance and wordlessly relive it, incredulous that the human who went away and did those things could now be here trying to tell it. And then he'd pick up again, like Atlas, invigorated by the time-out. When would he be back? I'd completely forgotten. Was he in New Zealand or Fiji? Only time would tell, via him.

Atlas was heartier now, funk-free, and regaling (if that's the word) me with talk of Mercury (Merc, he said, again, or Herm) who sometimes doubled, stood in, for the evening star, always kept his face toward you, and wobbled a bit like Dr. Johnson. In recent times he'd developed some curious discolorations down one side, a kind of planet-impetigo, weepy and atingle. Maybe a new mode of growth, Atlas suggested: the effect of the sun's getting gradually hotter and bigger. Or maybe some parasitism, where panspermia had touched him. All that was certain was that one day, in say about eight billion years ("How'd you like that to be the unserved portion of your sentence?" Atlas asked with grim jocosity), the Sun would become a red giant, engulf both Mercury and Venus, and its surface would approach the orbit of Earth. "Then it'll all be over," laughed Atlas. "*You'll* have fried long before that! No doubt to hearten himself during these morbid sallies, he chanted a little tune, the words of which ran thus:

"He-he, h-h, H Ca, Mg Ca, Fece." What it meant, I have no idea, and he refused to tell; but the last word sounded oddly like 'fecal,' though I'm sure it wasn't that at all. The second sound was merely a double aspirate, which he carried over to the third, and the effect of hearing my own voice reiterate this from the cassette was weird and sinister. *Hcmgcfca*, I fast-thought: maybe it's Lincos, the language for interstellar communication invented by the Dutch mathematician Hans Freudenthal (sometimes my TV-viewing pays off in extraordinary ways). Asked, Atlas poo-poohed the notion, wouldn't tell ("You'd never understand," he said), and instead, swung off into what I can only describe as a virtuoso piece, airing not so much his knowledge as, mirrorwise, my own ignorance (TV or not). "Take T Tauri stars, for example. Photographed in red light, they can be caught actually ionizing the gas in their vicinity, thus creating what shows up, believe it or not, as a silver lining. Beautiful! As for panspermia, which we were discussing only a moment ago, if the Earth had been seeded some billions of years ago, the initial germ must've been ejaculated from a star not more than six thousand light years away. If that doesn't make you think, nothing will." Then he rambled off into something about "hydrogen spinflip" and being slapped in the face when very young for miscounting the petals on a flower. Whence, no doubt, his hostility to education. Or to its process, at least. For long spells, he claimed, he'd had no fun at all, so he'd wept for joy in 1054, on the Fourth of July in fact, when a Class I supernova in Taurus exploded, astonishing the Japanese and the Chinese although apparently not the Europeans. A star which had previously been quiet and well-behaved burned so bright that it was visible even in the daytime. "Debris now known," he said complacently, "as the Crab Nebula, now expanding at six hundred and eighty miles per second!" Solar flares he'd kind of gotten accustomed to, of course, but 1898 hadn't been too bad, that being the year of Asteroid Eros, fifteen miles long and five wide, the first asteroid to pass inside Earth's orbit. Then, in 1957, Comet Mrkos had cheered him up no end, with its solar windsock tail. "It's like," he explained, "seeing an occasional bit of baseball, huh?

After the Greeks, see, there were only the Romans, and after them there was no more mythology. Things kind of slowed down, like the universe one day will. Ha, I recall the scheme labelled Project Ozma, supposed to detect interstellar radio signals of intelligent origin, if any! Well, they laid the 27-meter Green Bank antenna on two stars, Epsilon Eridani and Tau Ceti, in 1960, Fall through Christmas, I believe, and got nothing at all. 'Eleven years ago, on those two stars,' each being about eleven light years distant, the project-director told the American Astronomical Society, 'it was pretty dull.' Well, Thor, my friend, it's been pretty dull here too since the beginning, since the Bang, El Grando Detonation! Yes sir, quiet to beat the band."

"I thought you said earlier," I heard myself objecting, "you believed in the Steady State theory."

"I believe in both," Atlas said, not without malice. "When I want to window-dress my own performance, I'm a Steady man; when I feel neurotic, I'm Bang. Simple, huh?"

Quite irresponsibly, at that point I cried for help. "Atlas, that isn't being fair. Don't you think I've heard about the universe's being made up of billions of galaxies and that they're systematically receding from one another like raisins in an expanding pudding? Isn't that so?" Told to eat my own pudding and like it (the alternative being, he said, an endless journey into and out of a Klein Bottle, which has neither inside nor outside), I decided to try to shift him back to family matters; but he wouldn't touch them, said instead what I wrote down as "Wons Wiki One."

"Hey," I blurted. "You're going too fast. Give me time to get things down."

"I thought you were just parroting them onto tape."

I told him there were one or two things I wrote down, either to keep my hands busy or, more probably, because I concentrated better when doodling, etc. He spelled it out. "You got it wrong, Thor. Sometimes I can receive visual signals. It's 1 Zwicky 1, the brightest object known. OK?"

I don't know about OK, but writing it down again, during the perfunctory lull of transcription, I know I've got it right this time. Or was he, as sometimes, joking, being titanically snide? Had he, or had he not, somewhere in all this told me, when he was unduly piqued with my slowness or my denseness, told me to shunt off? And had I told him to do the same, at once adding, "No, please *don't!*"? Something of the kind must have taken place (though it isn't in the tape), for I distinctly recall his saying, "If I do, it'll be into the world's largest radio dish, the Arecibo radio-telescope of Cornell University, in Puerto Rico, three hundred meters across." It almost sounded as if he meant he'd *relieve* himself into it, monstrous thought from which I shrank. Or have I imagined all this, in white heat of vicarious fervor? As if driving at speed toward another car on a night highway, cursing the other man's brights, when all the time it's a mirror some prankster has erected in the road. (Or some civic official, hell-bent on making the town look twice as big.) Do I, in discovering Atlas, uncover myself, become indecent? It was little use asking *him*, I'd have only confused the issue further, as if saying to myself: Does the act of asking yourself who you are make you a preciser being than you were before? Or merely muzzier? Balderdash to all that. Time I got back to the old drawing board. When Atlas speaks again, it will not be to fall silent; I need my wits about me, peace of mind, some extra supplies of sherry, and, above all, some fresh tapes, *tabulae rasae* for him to deface.

2.
Tan Salaam

(Brain Stem: in evolutionary terms, an old and primitive part)

*H*is name is Tan Salaam, self-bestowed since he was dismissed from the Tanzanian civil service for illegally dealing in four elephant tusks. What his former name was I neither know nor care, I am too taken by his gleaming ebony face, the aloof equanimity in his eyes, the hair circlet around his shaven head. He looks not so much African as Oriental, not so much disgraced as called to a higher service. A candy-striped sheet wound round his trunk serves him as skirt, and an ordinary drip-dry shirt, several sizes too large, covers his upper body. Round his neck there is what once might have been a scarlet cummerbund, now faded into a bleached-looking pink, and his wrists are thin enough to fit into aluminum bracelets sliced from (I think) a Coca-Cola can, one on each. Off him comes an aroma I am not familiar with, a sweet stench that is pine and baby's diaper mixed. His nails are long enough to scoop out the contents of an egg and he has two moustaches, a conventional one along his upper lip and a surprising one beneath his lower lip: a mouth rimmed with fur.

"The matter of the tusks," I say.

"Greed," he answers, "which I have now put behind me, but with gratitude, for the tusks led me to my life's work. An augury, I think you would call it. You cannot learn anything without first submitting to disgrace, not that I had any such thing in mind when I began dealing in ivory. Far from it, but the privilege crept up on me. I was even unwilling. Nonetheless, I was *called* without asking for anything remotely similar, and now I am transformed. I am earlier, so to speak, than all priests, having no necessary doctrine; I am quite empirical, in that I rely upon experience only, and such experience as quite overwhelms; and I am, let's face it, wholly outrageous in that I excite just as much hate as admiration. According to my log, well over four thousand pilgrims have come to visit me, some of them even driving up in their Land Rovers while on safari. To them I am a curiosity, but one that lingers in their minds; to others, adepts who might also have been to Tibet or Benares, I am an inspiration. For some time, after my downfall—which I now have come to regard as an essential step in my initiation—I wandered about the parklands, cursing their Director, a one-time big-game hunter turned conservationist, and resolving to have my revenge. I would, I told myself, turn ivory trader in a big way. Months I spent in such futile bickering with myself, almost like Job, and then, one day of unusual heat even for these treeless grasslands, I happened upon—no, that isn't the way to express it—I saw from a distance something that looked like a tall building, say the Post Office tower in London, or the United Nations Building in New York City, an eminence in a land where eminences are few and far between. So, naturally, I stopped, attributing the whole thing to a mirage, something brought on by a near-starvation diet and the fatigue of walking day after day. But the image didn't vanish; from about one hundred yards, if you allow for the shimmer of the heat on the land, it looked gray, shall I say granitic."

"Like a puy," I learnedly interject, "or a menhir. A dolmen has two or more upright columns.

"As you prefer," he says smoothly. "So I approached, half-expecting the thing to disappear. But it didn't, and then I heard the buzz-buzz which you yourself hear at this very moment, and I apologize for that. Thousands of flies, like pursuit planes circling one of your skyscrapers. And a stench like the amalgamated sewers of all the cities in West Africa. To the touch it wasn't hard at all, nor yet soft, but buoyant like densely packed straw. What I had been drawn toward was a thirty-foot pile of elephant dung, assembled there for no reason I could even faintly imagine.

He leans forward toward the telephone on his trestle table and rests his chin on the base of his hand; the aluminum bangle slides down his arm half-way. (The phone will never ring for it is unconnected.)

"At first," he goes on, "I imagined some human agency had put it all there for collection later—some new technique of making bricks, say, or a special load for one of the universities where they study conservation so relentlessly. But then I realized it had been amassed by the elephants themselves, shoving and heaving at the heap and then lobbing chunks of the stuff up higher and higher, and they smoothed the column with their trunks. It was as if they were erecting a cenotaph, something to compete with Kilimanjaro, or an elephant *kopje*, a parody of our small hills with granite boulders. And I told myself: Tan Salaam (although that wasn't my name then), you have been granted a mighty privilege. This is not just a dungheap of the elephants, it is a beacon, a pillar, a platform crying out for a Simon Stylites to mount it. Imagine the humility I had arrived at! Imagine the arrogance as well! Perhaps, I told myself, the elephants would return and knock it down. On the other hand, perhaps they had erected it to show that I, and only I, was forgiven— provided, of course, that I did penance on that very spot. It was no doubt a reckless decision to make, but it wasn't a chance I was willing to forego."

"But," I protest, "aren't there laws? Weren't there all kinds of practical difficulties? I mean, what about food and water, what about human contact?"

He looks amused: "It was right in the middle of the Serengeti, where you are allowed to destroy nothing, where all life is sacred. Everything is protected there, even a hill of elephant dung. And so it turned out. Plus the fact of the tourist trade, rising fifteen percent annually if I remember aright. All I had to do was situate myself on top of the pile and the tourists would come. And a few devout followers would bring food and water, which they do. In fact, I have been up here for going on four years; my feet in all that time have not touched the earth once. The telephone! I see you glancing at it, as if you expect it to ring. To me, it is a symbol of useless communication. See (he holds up the receiver), I eat from it (the earpiece and mouthpiece are hollowed out to form minor cups).

"Here, the water," he says, "there the food. I take in little, barely enough to keep body's rental paid, but I am well known for that. It would be too late to change now."

As if for the first time, I realize that, contrary to all my expectations, I am sitting on a cushion made of soft branches on top of a thirty-foot high pillar of dung in the center of the Serengeti grasslands, conversing with a self-made shaman, both of us almost enclosed in outsize flies and breathing almost pure stench in 120-degree heat. I marvel at man's power to adjust.

"*Tan Salaam*," I say, formally, "what does *that* mean?"

"Oh," he says, affably, "that is a pair of local allusions—to the Tan in Tanzania, patriotic, you see, and to the Salaam—Arabic for peace—in Dar-es-Salaam, the capital. I call this the Peace Turret, and, if you will take the trouble to look down, through the flies, you will see something else."

I do, but I don't believe it. Picture, if you will, a sailboat with green and white sail planked there in the middle of nowhere, no water in sight, with lions and zebras and buffaloes and giraffes and leopards and wildebeests and cheetahs and wild dogs and vultures and so on daily going past it, leaving it alone. It is as if a TV commercial has come home to roost: "Special bargain covers delivery of a complete sailboat (pictured at right)—

Now I know where I have seen it, not on TV, but in some illustrated magazine bought at a newsstand near the Chicago Loop.

"—including thirty-pound molded polystyrene hull, aluminum mast and spars, forty-five square-foot nylon sail, fittings, lines, rudder, centerboard and sailing instruction booklet.

Allow six weeks for delivery. This offer expires December 31, 1971, is limited to the USA., and is open only to those 21 years of age or over. . . . I enclose a carton end flap from any size (some cigarette, I forget which) plus $88."

"The Sea Kite," I say to him. "I've seen them!"

"From an American admirer," he tells me. "He brought it with him on his second visit. I stare at it and it helps my mind to lift. You see, there is a special point to its presence: this is one of the world's oldest continuously inhabited regions, so it is worth seeing how long it survives. So far, the only force to affect it has been the sun. It is two years old, it has been nowhere, of course, but it remains intact.

"Beautiful," I exclaim. What *else* can one say?

Agreeing, he offers me food, some kind of mash, but not in the telephone cup, not in either of them but in a dull-looking can that might once have contained soup.

"No thank you; it is as much as I can do to breathe up here. A green air of Africa, thirty feet up, with nary a breeze!"

"But the smell," I begin to ask.

"I do not even notice it. Too, I accept the flies."

"Your own—"

"With my own paltry droppings, I add to the mound. Shall we say a yard nearer heaven each year? I concede the crudeness of the platform, but I allow three or four tents down below in which my so-called followers can live. At the moment, I am quite alone; I have more visitors at weekends, and then I unroll this."

He fidgets with some strings and pegs, and a ten-foot-square banner on what looks like a tablecloth unrolls and settles. Peering over, I see a cross superimposed upon a swastika, black on grimy white.

"My emblem," he explains." "I also have a small handbell (he rings it eerily in the chaffering stillness of the grassland) and a book to write in (a brown-bound spiral exercise book)."

At once he begins to read to me from it, but not before I see that the writing is copperplate, in brown fiber-point:

In two-score months and nine I have not bathed.
So: I have lost a tooth, my hair has grown gray,
and, lean and black as a hyena ravaged by hunger,
I am covered with scabies. Fortunately,
Being a stubborn and stoical man, never yielding,
Though I suffer in the body,
My spirit stands firm.

He must surely, I reflect, have read Ho Chi Minh's prison diary, and I wonder at his opportunism, ask him. No, he says, young men from America have climbed the ladder and read it to him, he regrets any seeming plagiarism.

"Do you, then," I ask him, "have a creed? Do you propound beliefs that people can follow? Put into practice."

"None at all. Merely contemplation and meditation."

"A life of inaction?"

"Precisely."

"Any day an elephant, even a herd of them, could bulldoze you down."

"Thus far, my son, they have not."

"And that is the essence of what you do?"

"Their peace toward me, mine toward them. As well as all other creatures. The government indulges me: I am what is known as a tourist draw; I cost the government nothing; I harm nobody. I am picturesque."

"Money?"

"I accept none, but only supplies. An occasional piece of soap, a toothpick, any kind of food."

"But the heat? It almost has me fainting."

"One adjusts." (I thought he was going to call me son again, but he doesn't.)

"And the point is peace?"

"Not the word, but the experience of being vulnerably on top of a large amount of what most people would think disgusting. I think peacefully while nature piles up."

"Ah, then the elephants do not return?"

"Not one ounce have they added. No, as I see it, the heap is complete; all it lacked was a tenant. Perhaps there are similar peace turrets all over the Serengeti, which is very vast, and I have not seen all of it."

"Will you ever come down?"

"When death brings me."

"What about family?"

"My wife in the capital city divorced me for desertion. An epiphany, you realize, is a lonely thing."

Dust in the distance attracts my eyes and he motions toward it: More visitors, he coos, almost implying I have to go.

"So, peace is here?"

"Isn't it?"

"I'm sorry, it all seems so contrived."

"As you wish. Spiritual beggars cannot be choosers. Imagine how I would feel if my destiny had been to sit in a burned-out Rolls-Royce in a suburb of Dar-es-Salaam, eventually doomed to douse myself with gasoline and become a human torch! My version is an *African* otherworldliness; it was Nature who provided my platform. With Nature I will stay."

Among other things, he tells me about helicopters that come to hover above him while tourists spin their movie cameras; vultures that greet him, so he says, with a concerted flap of wings during helices of squadron drill; lions that pause at the Sea Kite and bass-purr in greeting; the London journalist who wrote an article about him that he never saw; the honorary degree he eventually expects from one of the major African universities; the mild pain in his groin that might be a grumbling appendix; the days the blue of the sky seems to drain his eyes completely and he can discern, although only behind closed lids, while tiny cells flit across the irradiated screen of blood, the radar octopus of heaven, the all-registering. I, I look for the mouths of whiskey bottles embedded in the dried dung, for some sign of supplementary rations. Are none. He's true to what he says. Even giraffes don't molest him. Out there, he isn't even insanitary, only the exhaust of the Land Rovers and the minibuses. Unlike St. Paul, he wasn't called to service by fulguration, he just loitered around and struck gold. I prepare to go, eyes tingling with sweat's salt, throat parched, clothes sodden, and head pounding from the glare, even through the polaroid lenses.

"Remember," he says as I prepare to go down the rickety ladder, "as many as forty thousand animals a year are poached in Tanzania's parks. A good zebra skin will fetch thirty to forty dollars, a leopard's up to two hundred. Peace isn't easily come by. A lioness has three or four cubs every two years, and if they all survived, there would be an unequal balance of lions to wildebeests, which have only one calf each year. So nature kills off some of the lion cubs, two or three of which can eat an entire gazelle in three or four days. Normally, the gazelle would have seven years of life. Some things are intended, others not. How long a stack of dung can last, nobody knows; perhaps this one is the first of many. Who knows? I intend to sit it out."

"Anything I can get for you?" I feel contrite at being still suspicious. What about laundry? Surely he shaves?

"The nights are cold," he answers; so, for them, I reserve warm thoughts—the daytime Serengeti; dreams of volcanoes; incendiary bombs on London; sun-bursts, high fevers.

Nodding, even though he cannot see me, I stand again on the braised ground, then walk away to my own Land Rover. There he squats, on his stout stem of shit, unassailable in his African paradoxes, his Eastern elasticity, his English-type education that has fed him all the right words. It is as if he rides on a private Golden Fleece, trusting in the winds to land him in one piece, if ever. I have no doubt that, after five or ten or twenty years, if the dungheap endures, the vultures will one day topple his skeleton off the platform, but not until then will he touch the ground. Anyone who needs him will have to go up.

3.
Captain Ahab:
A Novel by
the White Whale

I too, alone, survived to tell thee. A whale tells this, white as Biscay froth, a tale black as caviar. I almost lost heart. Albinos do, doomed special while feeling like the rest. We're dark unto ourselves. *We*? I am the only one. I have never bred. I have never seen a white male or a white mate. I never had company save for him. Only, during brief heaven, a mother who nudged and nourished. Shunned, I go from ocean to ocean, falling in love with icebergs and fluffy fog, and, nearer shore, with snow and polar bears. I am forbidden nothing, but there is nothing I can have. What sex am I? Did Ahab know?

Squinting aft, I see him, rib cage and all. As the years went by, he began to rattle, then to chime. I read his last will and testament from his lips, then took him down for the count, poor piscuniak of a mariner. Then I whale-hummed at him, just to be friendly. I wanted somehow to swing him loose, then pop him down, minnow-small and feather-frail. Install him on the bulby mound of one vast kidney according to Jonah Law. A pet, a familiar, a love.

But dislodge him I could not, and I soon knew his coming for what it was: a test in the form of a sign, a sign in the form of a test. Could I brook his presence without wanting friendship? Ahab was my birthmark. Yes. "Ishmael, art thou sleeping there below?" Then answer would come: "Moby, I am thine, for ever."

It was all hopeless. Call me, I began, but my still-thundering jelly of a heart floated upward through my mouth, jump-a-thump, and all that's left is an infolded compass-rose, miming its thanks, murmuring a dew.

4.
How to Marry a Hummingbird

Cynthia Dougherty hated afternoons. Florida ones were the worst and this was the worst of those. She had to get through it, but she couldn't repeat the best trick she had thought of yet. She had, on that occasion, written down on a letter card most of the possible permutations of her husband's Social Security number and mailed it to him at the air base annotated, in grandiloquent banality, "From one of me to all of you." It had baffled Rob, who began baffled anyway, and she felt that somehow she had refined his mental predicament while dignifying her own. If only, he'd said, she had kept it until the evening—the card, of course. She thought of her bikini pictures and cutting out the clothed parts to send him, saying, "From the best of me," but she abandoned the idea. The afternoon was too hot for anything ingenious.

Stacked neatly in a minor architectural complex on the blazing face of her petit-point looking glass, the apparatus of calm awaited her need. The cylinder of suntan spray towered over her Winstons, the neatly folded book of matches called "Surefire," a pair of parchment-colored ear plugs, and one pack of gum with the red ribbon partly peeled away. She did some visual mental arithmetic, then checked the numbers by saying them aloud. It was probably the twelve thousand, seven hundred and eightieth afternoon of her life on earth.

Since one-thirty she had been idling on the baked lawn and wincing at the summer calls and incessant swooping curves of the backyard birds. Having slept only one hour the previous night she had the dazed, rebuffed feeling of not being within the envelope of her own body. She felt as if she were lying beside herself about three feet away; and beside herself also, she noted, in womanish rage. It had been Rob. Why any light colonel should spend four hours between midnight and light explaining, or rather shirking explaining, why he wasn't going to be promoted was beyond her. He had sat in the living room, occasionally getting near the point but then drifting off into the preliminaries of yet another deliciously confessed infidelity while she patted his knees or stood up and went to do superfluous polishing in the kitchen. Almost a whole bottle of bourbon had enriched his mumblings but had not blocked the usual résumé of his wasted life: the guilt about the saturation bombing he was decorated for doing in Europe, the guilt of skimming the girls of fifteen nations and having affairs, the guilt of telling her (who stood by him), the guilt of no longer wishing to touch her, the guilt of not pretending about that ("I could've, I could've, but I couldn't"), the guilt of—oh, just too much talk about guilt. They had gone to bed without even a curt goodnight, he to immediate drunken insensibility, she to a clock-watching, irritable vigil. Brian the boy, the four-year-old, always woke at six-thirty and pummeled her until she woke. He never had to pummel much.

For about a year this had been the pattern of two nights in five, and she had long known Rob would not be promoted: he was willfully insolent to superior officers. He got away with it; but getting away with it, as she told him, was getting nowhere. He had now applied for Vietnam in the hope, he said, of being killed, as he should have been during the war. It was either that or going back into the Church, which he had left informally in 1940. And there was guilt of that too. That was the guilt he enjoyed most.

"Look, Rob," she had insisted, "the war is over. Done. No, don't touch me. The bombs have *fallen*, you don't *have* to tell me about these girls," and then shouting, "I don't *want* to know!" Her voice had echoed out into the fetid, insecticidal-perfumed night. The ground-spraying vehicle had just gone past, and the air reeked of DDT that stung the eyes delicately and dried her voice into a shrill.

He had a long drink then. "Tar*ew*, hon'," he said slowly, meditatively, "but it brings us close. When I tell you, I mean. You listen and then I know it's all all right. Don't go," as she rose and made for the kitchen, there to renew her diet cola. "Don't walk out—just listen, don't talk. Hon'?"

She leaned round the half wall, stared him full in the eyes (he was twisting his neck to see her) and whispered percussively that she didn't want to listen. She was going to bed. "Talk," she opened her mouth wide as if preparing to receive a whole apple, "to yourself." Then she accidentally caught her glass against the wall. He laughed because he heard it smash against the simulated marble floor. She retrieved some pieces and threw them with short-distance violence into the gaping trash can; the lid had stuck as if giving a Nazi salute.

They always quarreled in such formulas as these. Their dispute had no heart in it but resolved itself into a verbal quadrille while each of them thought privately about other matters: Rob of the girl pick-up he had given money to for some minor operation, Cynthia of all the places she had been posted to with him and the long solitary nights she had spent in Rome, Oxfordshire, and Turkey (to name a few) reading those interminable Tolstoys and retreating into the too-soon-finished Spillanes. Words bounced between them, occupying the space but never reducing it. Last night his thickly fleshed face had gone beet-red and the sweat had beaded down from his sideburns while he toyed with the slight lever of his fly zip. It had gone on, neither of them feeling capable of breaking the pattern. After all, she mused, it was the only intimate bond they had remaining to them. Without it he would have cried and drunk more bourbon, and she, narrow and slender, chronically attuned to his moods and tics, would have lost a pose in which she saw herself, in wan hyperbole, as a hummingbird and even felt the part in her garish kimonos. She laughed at such an idea: it was fanciful and silly, not a grown woman's thought at all. But, strained and set quivering and given enough stimulus to self-pity, she let the thought in and watched herself vibrating in the night. "How," she thought, "you mate a hummingbird. Only a few know. Keep her in motion all night, wings whirring like mad, and above all don't let her escape to some other place or room where she might have a life that isn't all words and quarrels and hollow making-up (on lucky nights) just before dawn, always in words, but never through a real hard. . . ." Her head felt twice its normal weight as she sat down again on the floor beside his chair and let her hand float up to his. He was still in the pants of his uniform. Bourbon had stained the front, and her damp palm left a faint, balanced print on the fabric. "Use the glass," she admonished as he reached for the bottle, "use the glass. Don't lose your manners too."

Out on the lawn she made a deliberate, fist-clenching effort to stop remembering. She shook her head to dislodge the memory of the night and felt the steam-heavy air cling to her face before slumping away. "God," she thought, "I'm losing contact with *everything*. How do you stay sane all day with only a child to talk to?" She looked round for Brian, and not seeing him, sang messages through her nose in case he was near: "Brian, honey, don't you go too far away. You hear me now. Stay close to the house and close the refrigerator door if you use it. No, not *use*; *open* it." Then she thought herself ridiculous, screaming self-corrections the boy was bound to misunderstand. But she had breath left, tension still not dispelled. So: "You hear me, lover?" Lover was not answering.

Only that morning, while she squeezed his orange for him, he had asked in his direct, ingenuous way, "Mom, is it this day or the next day?" She had reassured him it was today, Wednesday, but he hadn't seemed convinced, because he then accused her of "putting him on." So she threatened him with Sunday school; she would make this day Sunday and not a next day, which meant he would have to go and be like Jesus for two whole hours. That beat him. He drank his orange juice in a puzzled, metaphysical silence, committed to this day above all others and determined to be bad when she fell unwakably asleep as she always did in the afternoon.

The pool filter choked, then wheezed again into life. She was just going to call Brian again when she caught sight of him asleep, indolently plunged on a rubber mattress in the corner of the patio, the wet glistening on his back like snail's tracks. He was dreaming, she told herself, about invisible invaders he had killed or repelled with his spacegun until only a few minutes ago. It was now about three; her glance at her wrist didn't even take in the minute hand, and she wondered why she bothered to wear her watch. Her stomach told her the time. She scowled and picked up the suntan spray from the withered grass. The jet felt cool against her arms and legs. All she could hear was the pool filter, the canary from inside, the refrigerator hum and the *pss-pss* of the spray as she squirted. She lay down, rolling the back of her head to make a hollow in the blanket. The spray can felt like a hot-water pipe in her hand, so she let it fall. The afternoon had to be got through somehow. What could she do? A drink? No, that would just renew last night. She couldn't go and talk to Adèle next door because Adèle, fresh from Montreal on a permanent visa so she could obtain her divorce, had taken her three pampered children on a motor yacht with her boyfriend, the attorney from Washington who was down on a visit. Gorgeous, giggling, bird-of-paradisey, dynamic Adèle, who called her "Cyn" with a soft "C" and taught her how to use a lipstick brush, had deserted her, and with her had gone the funnel-shaped, floppy, ever-willing ears into which "Cyn" had slid the diffident rancor of the past four months while aching, ever so little, to touch her new friend, the broadness of her, the hard pulp of the calves, the nervous discolored lids of her narrow green eyes.

"No, I'm *not* that kind of woman," she had told herself when reviewing things one raining day, "I just love my friend. If that's a crime, or a kink . . ." Adèle had a college degree and talked about recessive genes. Rob always watched her, pushing his tongue under his right upper lip. Adèle had told her to refuse him, not to listen to his confessions. "It's a luxury for him; like my ex-to-be. Don't listen to him, and he'll like you again. You'll see." Cynthia had tried it and

Robert hadn't come home for a week, although he had called her from North Carolina, affectionately too. But when he did come back he didn't touch her at all. And then Adèle had told her what to do next, but Cynthia hadn't followed or even wanted to follow. One morning, while making the instant at coffee time, she had asked Adèle again, but Adèle for once seemed out of counsel. "It's a young body he wants," Cynthia had announced, "it's the young body. He thinks he's getting old. And being with me makes him older than ever." Adèle had nodded, poking in her ear with a bobby pin as if truth had lodged in the cavity.

Now Cynthia was lying at peace, her veined, undernourished-looking legs crossed and her arms extended at right angles. She was prone and would be so for roughly ten minutes before going supine again with the same pattern of limbs. At least the birds, cawing and quarreling, made no demands. The grass was over ankle height; one hinge of the flimsy back-yard gate was broken, and children had been infiltrating. A decomposing cardboard box brought sometime from the liquor store reposed at an angle on the crowded dandelions, announcing "Straight Bourbon Whiskey 86 Proof" although they had brought home only two bourbon and six bottles of Chianti. She had tried to wean him onto wines, but the Chianti was still in the kitchen cupboard. An alien ball, more or less green, and a foot in diameter, was perched on top of the arbor. She cursed then, the broken power mower, her husband's indolence (he could bomb but not fix), the casual habits of the garbage men, and the inaccuracy of ball-tossing children. Then she felt able to relax.

She lay musing, mostly on her name and its odd beginning. Not the Cynthia part, as that was birthright and sacrosanct, a possession for which everyone respected her; but the "Dough" in Dougherty, as if she had caught on too late and discovered her spouse was a baker. But that was better than starting too early and thinking, on the strength of "Do," that he was a man of action, and then getting bogged down in "ugh."

Starting later in the name she found "erty" a cheering compensation, dismissing "dirty" and the vulgar "purty" and concentrating on the way it thinned out the "Dough," stretched it out, turned it from loaf into *baguette*, from squat plebeian into long and thin and delicate-grained aristocratic bread fingers. Then she remembered how everyone said the word with a Scottish *ch* as in *loch*; she thought of phlegm—not cheerful imperturbability but expectoration on buses—and she wished with all her heart she could be just Cynthia.

Tiny gray insects kept settling on her arms. She dislodged them, but they kept returning. The faint down of her outer arms failed to trap or repel them, and when she was supine they landed on the unbrowned skin of her inner arm as if landing on silk. They nuzzled and bit. Again she flailed, and soon she was walking irritably about the small garden walled in by foliage and teased by the birds. She stood and attended: one bird threatened in a high, spinning snarl; another muttered from ground level in widely spaced single pleas—like vocal hyphens; and others, all of a kind, contended in tiny hysterical hisses.

Before she knew it she was stroking a nettle, safely, in the direction of the spines. Thrilled in a small way to be trifling with danger like this, she thought of her collections indoors of birds' eggs, butterflies, pressed flowers, and unusual stones. Their bedroom was full of boxes, full of her various collections. She dusted them every morning before dusting the rest of the house. The fragile hollow shells gleamed with her love; the wings of the pinned butterflies seemed grateful for reprieve from endless undulation; the flowers gladly gave up the stale chore of contracting and closing, opening and expanding; and the stones, she felt, dimly but positively, knew they were safe. The nettle obeyed her coaxing hand; there was no sting. But she was standing. She went indoors, past Brian, dragged out a collapsible chair and brought it to the spot where the nettles grew. Then she sat, reaching out again for the leaf, stroking it again and again until there seemed a current between her cupped fingers and its rough undersurface. Then, for no good reason, she lit a Winston and held the match flame under the leaf. The leaf lay still; the flame fattened and reached upward; the rim of the leaf curled and crouched, and then the flame began to sear her finger. She waved her hand against the humid air, as if snubbing and dismissing whole crowds of people.

The afternoon had still to be got through. When Rob was home she asked, "Is this all there is?" When he was away she asked, "What am I supposed to do with peace anyway?" They had been married eight years, and when she surveyed the chaste shimmer of the kitchen or the geometrical repose of the living room she was glad. But in the bathroom, alone with a fragrant soap called Harem and mingled scents of shaving lotion and instant lather, as well as the fur of towels drying in the direct light, she hated the throat-urging, disrupting tickle of small stools come upon in the pedestal after the boy had raced out to play. Again she stroked the nettle, caressing it and winning over all the capacity of the world to hurt: the unyielding needles, the bloodsucking clocks, the soured elations, the wasted vows, the constant menace of roaches, the untidy weather, the trouble on the lawn and in the bed, the way friends went off, the child slept, the match burned her, the gum dried or softened, the way—the silly, showing-off way—Rob upset the boy, trying to make him —well, somehow rough. Brian was not only a boy: he was the king of the boys, as well as the king of the gorillas, dinosaurs, mountain climbers, monster-killers, spacemen, and underwater long-distance swimmers. He was (and this Rob sang like Popeye) Brian the Lion, and would give this title when asked who he was.

So, while Cynthia tried to interest the boy in her collections, which he liked in any case, Rob the father encouraged him to accept a grandiose domestic reputation. But when Brian told his friends of his prodigious roles in jungle and space, in swollen rivers and at anoxic altitudes, they jeered, and he wondered how to prove the truth. He was trapped between losing face with his friends, of whom he had few, being shy, and refusing his father's worship. He was baffled and upset to be king of so uncomprehending, so badly informed a world; and the more baffled he became, and the more upset, the more his father fed him with myths entailing the crossing or purging of crocodile-infested rivers and the quick dispatch of arrogant giants. The more inept the boy felt when confronted with his growing reputation, the more his father made him a superman. Sometimes, at the mention of giants or monsters, Cynthia screamed, predicting for her son a colossal complex and a short, unheroic life in which he wouldn't even have time to learn how to blow an egg. But the boy stared and Rob guffawed her into silence. Then the heroic interlude went on while she retired to tidy her collection boxes.

On a sudden whim she went in, checking to see that the front door was locked. It wasn't and it wouldn't lock. Another thing to be fixed. Twenty-first Street North sailed neatly before her, quelled by the summertime and trimmed daily by careful, evening men with hoses, small knives, and pots of weedkiller. Crabgrass had no future here. The road shimmered and waited. She turned away, grimaced at the mess of her sodden hair in the mirror, and then walked, as if into a waterfall, into the first ring of the phone. As if the instrument itself had been dozing and she woke it. The sound set her trembling.

"Hel—" she cleared her throat. "Hello?" It had been hours since she had spoken.

"Rob. I'll be home early, Momma. I want to talk. I mean I think *we* should talk. About last night—this morning." He sounded hoarse and quite convincing, she thought.

"Please yourself. I can't stop you. I can't make you come and I sure as hell can't make you go. Come or go." She had not realized she had had even that many words in her this afternoon. "If you want. You'll probably forget anyway soon as you've had a drink. I don't see why you couldn't have said what you want to say last night. No, I don't. Look, don't interrupt, please. I got no sleep. I feel dead. I don't want to talk to anybody, you least of all. I don't really want to listen either because the more I listen the worse you get. No, it's the truth. Honest. You do. You go and do something—anything, any *aw*ful thing—just so you can come home or come back and tell me about it, and I don't, do not, repeat don't, *want to know*. Not any of it. If it's something new, then save it and spill it somewhere else where they don't care. I feel dead and I wish I were and . . . and—Just tell yourself I'm deaf."

She was out of breath, surprised, and faintly impressed by the amount and impetus of her indignation. He had tried to interrupt, and she had overridden him each time. But he would come anyway and he would talk. If she avoided him all evening and went to bed early, he would wreck some other night. Perhaps that would be better; always later, better. "Please yourself. You always do, I couldn't care, I feel just absolutely—" It was the absoluteness of blankness, for she couldn't finish the sentence. He asked about the boy, but it sounded as if he were asking from the radio mast of some ocean liner thousands of miles off, inching gently toward an exotic coast of pink castles, cool courtyards, and dark, dashing, olive-skinned, undrunk men.

"He's fine." She wrenched the comment from the side of her mouth, glancing involuntarily through the large window that flanked the pool and wouldn't close properly. "He's asleep." She heard a sentimental grunt, a prediction that he would see her (that foolish idiom again, she winced), and then a sound as if the whole apparatus at the other end had fallen into an elevator shaft and life was extinct. She stared at the sweat marks, then killed the busy noise by sinking the receiver voluptuously back, the two rubber nipples being thrust home into the nostrils of the whirring animal. How she hated the phone with its demands on her voice. Your voice was never safe.

She went out again, unnerved. As quickly she came back. Then she went out again. She sat and stared at Adèle's washing as it swung minimally on the line. The small stringy plants by the house wall hunched and shivered as if some animal had blundered into them; but it was only the licking, furry July wind. Bees aimed at the flowers, found home, sucked dry, and reeled away like sailors. A black fly pestered her inner left ear until she flicked it away. She felt persecuted by miniature things. If only, she caught herself wishing, Rob were back. If only! She went silently hysterical at the thought. Then she had another thought and raced into the house, patio door clashing behind her, to take the phone off its cradle. The whine came at her unbroken, but it troubled her little. She felt as if she had turned on a dangerous jet of steam.

Moving to the lawn again she looked at Brian, black-haired, scowling, and sweating in his sleep. Gently, almost *en passant*—but she did linger a second or two—she raked her fingers across the velvet pad of his relaxed, bare belly, and he stirred, muttering. She clicked the patio gate behind her and again fell on the blanket. Her mind began to slow down. A few quiet moans later as if someone had intimately curled up with her, she fell asleep, sailing on another ocean this time, with a boatload of children who licked lollipops in tongue-tied unison.

She had been asleep only ten minutes when Brian stirred, shook himself like a wet puppy, and called, gently so as not to wake her, "Mom! Hey, Mom!" He half-smiled and sat up, gazing round the pool. He was safe, he knew. If any lion, or Monsky, the three-eyed monster with the machine gun sewn into his belly-button, should burst from the house, he, Brian, could be at her side in three steps. Then he went into the house, breathing heavily, stunning ogres with one glance from his electric eyes and burning guns from the very hands of hidden outlaws. He looked around, this time with his ordinary eyes. The house was untidy. He liked it neat, his heavy toys stacked right angle to right angle in the bottom of his toybox; then lighter things such as planes, small cars with fins, and pencil boxes. The heavy filling station was usually on the bottom, the lead soldiers and the plastic revolvers on top. He always set his comics in a gaudy block on top of everything. Today nothing was in place. So he set to and, after retrieving them, put his toys away, heedless of his possible needs in half an hour's time.

One day he had even tidied up the entire house, making the beds, washing down the patio, emptying the garbage, and collecting up the detritus of perhaps two days and fitting the orange peels, the matches from books of matches, empty cigarette packages, feathers, gum wrappers, fragments of toilet roll, small glasses that smelled of gasoline, pieces from hastily opened envelopes, fallen crumbs, and newly dead thousand-leggers. All this he had dropped into an old salt canister and tamped down with his clenched fist. Then he put the filled canister into the garbage can outside. Some days the house was neat in a military, hospital way; others it was a mess. Some days Cynthia let the mess accumulate, especially if she had had a bad night (two in five), and then like a Conquistador prevailed over the debris, reducing all to geometrical decency in a matter of hours. But Brian could never understand why all days were not alike. He liked the mess because he could tidy up; but he also liked the neatness because he knew where his toys were.

He went outside to the patio and slid down the steps into the water, holding on all the time. He felt cooler. Then he released his grip and leaned slowly forward, sinking to the bottom and lying there prone as if preparing to sleep. It was his newest trick and he practiced it for fifteen minutes or so, plunging up for air with his eyelashes stuck together into small black thorn shapes and his face pale green from the water.

When, for the first time, he threw his head back he saw the twig on top of the patio cage. It annoyed him and he stared at it, trying to melt it with a space stare. Then small rhomboids of light shuffling across the surface of the water caught his eye and, lower down, something else. He sank again to the bottom, his shape deformed by the depth. He groped, slowly, and then began to rise again until he burst from the water with wet seal's head and his mouth round as if someone had just unplugged a teat. Gasping and blinking he pushed aside a comical-faced red rubber mouse floating against his shoulder and looked at his hand. There, dull and green from immersion, was a cent, a penny. Without a sound he aimed and slung the penny at the twig on the patio roof. He missed and the penny fell to the bottom of the pool. A silver cigar-shape slid across the sky, the high upper sky, going south.

The twig stared at him, like the skeleton of some misguided, trapped rooster. After clambering up the filter unit in the back yard and getting nowhere at all, he fetched a box from the garage and set it up outside, but leaning against, the mesh of the patio wall. When he had climbed up, after one mishap in which the box keeled over and fell on top of him, he stood and stretched as high as he could. It was no use. He abandoned the box, jumped nimbly down, and ran to the garden gate. Cynthia's mouth was open for a quite audible snore, and the boy smiled, wondering what he could drop into it. The fence adjoining and supporting the gate was one of woven planks, woven inside, then outside, the square uprights. He soon gained the top of the fence and moved onto the top of the garden gate. From there it was an easy swing to the flat roof. All he had to do now was haul himself to the roof and shimmy across the empty bedroom to the screen over the patio and the pool. With small grunts he did this and tested the wire mesh with a soft hand. It held firm against his push. He moved off, crawling, trying the area before him until he reached the twig on the third section of mesh from the gate. Above him the sky blazed blue and the clouds had fled to the edges of the world. There was no jet and the canary was silent. The filter urged itself on, hoarse and tired-sounding.

He broke the mesh when he stood up. His squeal was simultaneous with his plunge head-first toward the water. The twig dropped into the pool and floated as if happy to land. Brian, however, stayed suspended, his foot caught against a loop of wire, so that his head swung a couple of feet above the water and his free leg swept the air groping for purchase. First his head swung round in an oval of panic, then in a faster oval of exploration which gave him no help. He waved his arms, trying to swing himself free. He was determined not to cry out and he had already bitten back the one involuntary sound that had begun. Calmer, he took a small time out to ease an itch in his groin, which he did none the less competently for being upside down; and then, being small and having suppressed any noise, he made water in his swimming trunks. The fluid trickled down from the fabric and the bow of white tape across his navel, some lodging there, and then across his chest to his chin where it dispersed.

Cynthia slept on, deeply into it now. Because he had been swinging about, Brian's foot began to bleed. The wire had cut his ankle, and the rent mesh was scissoring his upper middle foot. The blood dried in the searing light of the sun, only to flow again when he swung himself again in a vain effort to get free. Tiny spittle drifted into the pool and floated. Then a speck appeared on the ankle and touched the dried and the seeping blood. In the sky another speck appeared, stopped or appeared to stop, and slowly grew in size as it sank down. He felt a tickling and tried to kick, first with the trapped foot, then with the free one. The tickle continued. Then he tried to look upward but looked right into the sun and sank down again with a scorching retina image of the sun, the torn mesh, and the steel frame of the patio roof. He began to shiver.

A small black fly buzzed against his face and dive-bombed him from somewhere in the sun. Below him the water swirled and shifted, now achieving a faint meniscus, now going concave, but always hospital green and winking back at him when he blinked his tears away. No one came although the morning paper, delivered late, hit the front walk with a thump. He did not hear it and he could not have read it anyway.

The frail, nut-brown body dangled steady as a plumbline and seemed to lengthen in the shifting sunlight. His face grew mauve. On the line next door the dishcloths and towels dried and grew rigid. A sudden slight wind blew loose one corner of one panel of the patio door screen, and the loose corner flapped. In the house the refrigerator continued with its nasal hum and the canary began to sing again in an obbligato of brittle, high notes. From the surrounding houses came only the chirps and squeals of children being put to bed for naps or awakening; one child wailed lengthily until silenced by cooing ventriloquisms from a high female voice. Cars crunched on gravel and hurried by. One car, louder than the rest, had no muffler. The snort seemed to occupy the neighborhood even after the car had gone. Cynthia woke, relapsed, then woke again.

The pelican settled on the steel frame of the patio roof and arched its neck, surveying the distance. Then it poked its ungainly head into the rent in the mesh. After a pause, as if afraid of a trap, it nosed the boy's foot, which then scraped and slipped and silently fell downward, taking the stuck fruit flies with it after the body into the water. Cynthia heard the splash and screwed up her eyes against the sun. The pelican flew up in panic as the saw-teeth of water subsided and, circling once, batted its wings before seeking a current of air to idle on. The boy floated across the pool among the floats, plastic shells, and rubber animals.

Cynthia saw him, smiled, and stretched. Then she realized she had a beating headache and, while she was pondering the move to the house to find the right tablets, was amazed to see her son stumble up out of the pool, race to the patio door, and with a mounting scream run at her until he knocked her over, such was the force of his arrival. His foot was bleeding and he looked marble white or faint green. When she had calmed him in the house, he told her incoherently what had happened, and then she screamed too, stopping suddenly when she saw the boy begin to emulate her. She took him into his bedroom and sat with him after she dressed the cut on his ankle. There was no need to call a doctor.

Rob had parked his red MG with a declaratory "I'm-back" burst of the engine, hauled off his tie, and opened a can of Budweiser before he sensed anything different. He called loudly and heard a small response from the bedroom. When she told him, he stared woodenly, his head shifting forward, and suddenly raced out and jumped fully clothed into the pool, still holding the can of beer. He could think of nothing else to do. He could have done mouth-to-mouth on the boy, blowing the life into him, but there was no need of that. He insisted on calling a doctor, who came later that night and treated the ankle while Brian slept.

As all the implications of relief began to become real to them after the first, hallucinatory panic, they hesitated to look again at the living shape in the bedroom, primitively afraid it might rise up and strike them. As if he had been dead. Flies and moths poured through the hole in the patio roof; they filled the house, circling and squatting, bumping into eyes and flying into nostrils. The two of them sat unheeding. And while the boy rested in preparation for an even more marvelous tomorrow, she cradled Rob's head.

Next day he repaired the screen and drained the pool, thereby, she told him, making it even more dangerous. No, he told her; he had taken a day off and he had to do something. He spent the entire afternoon reading to the boy. Cynthia wept for most of the day but cheered up on a Martini about five. Brian fell asleep while watching a Western on the Early Show, and they both carried him in to bed, arranging his limbs with diligent, embalmer's care, and then rearranging until he half-woke and with sluggish petulance told them to lay off the blanket (which he called the "rampet"). They did, and then, over dinner, two TV dinners heated in recessed metal foil dishes, had a serious discussion.

Two nights later he touched her, and she wept with uncontrollable relief while he said something about "not leaving things to chance." When she told him, later that month, that she might be pregnant, he nodded several times and then laughed out loud. She bloomed and grew fey. He canceled his application for Vietnam. Brian found himself the recipient of many new toys. Adèle next door got her divorce but then told the judge she didn't want it and would he please not sign the papers; something had struck her, she said. Rob labored to be polite at the base; he even took Cynthia her breakfast in bed before he drove away in the mornings. And he began to cut down on the bourbon.

Their mutual reprieve lasted just over six weeks; and then she had to tell Adèle, still next door and beginning to dither again, "It's all started again, the same as before. Everything the same except it's worse now. I might have known, but I guess I didn't want to. So now what? Hey, Del?" Adèle's shrug said nothing. Adèle thought she had said enough, and Cynthia, in her slow-motion way, realized that nothing could be said. It was all beyond words, even beyond the sort of unspoken understanding they used to have. "I've tried," Cynthia told the blank TV screen, "I've tried too damn hard, just like I tried when I had Brian. Life's just one long squeeze—squeeze in, squeeze out, squeeze lemons, squeeze into clothes, cars, squeeze into *his* life—squeeze your courage or whatever it is. That's it: *screw* your courage. And as soon as something feels delicious, you look down and your fingers are all covered with slimy rotten banana. Well, I'm through with trying. It's time I did something else. Something for *me*."

Eventually, after a last two days of half-importunate tears

from her and bullish reassurances from him, he left in an Air Force car with what seemed to her fewer possessions than were seemly even for a light colonel (the levity of that went through her like a shiver of wind). She waved lamely from the walk, locked the repaired door, lifted the receiver off the phone, and went to join Brian in bed, where she slept with him in her arms until about three-thirty. Her last thought before dropping off was, "Oh Lord, he'll soon be in school—once August's done with."

By the time she woke, her mind was made up, like something left to bake while she slept. With Brian following her, meek with sleep, she walked into the patio in her yellow one-piece bathing suit, not even bothering to slip the straps over her sun-tender shoulders, and padded to the deep end of the empty pool. Abruptly she stabbed her head sideways in annoyance, then stared down at the concrete. "Oh, that'll never do. I'll kill myself." She went back to the sliding plate of glass which was both window and wall and stripped the long plastic cushion from the chaise, hauled it to the deep end and lowered it into the empty pool. "What do you do when you don't have stairs?" she asked herself as if in a trance. "What else?" Not even what she thought was the echo of her voice unnerved her. This was retaliation; a piece of her own back.

She stood, jumped, winced, trudged across to the ladder, pulled herself up the steps and walked back to jump again. Each time she jumped, Brian croaked with joy and clapped awkwardly. On she went: stand, jump, wince, cross the pool, climb up, stumble round; stand, jump again. The eighth or ninth jump did something, not to her numb feet, or her jellied knees and ankles, but to all of her trunk. She felt a vague, tidal churning and sank to her knees on the cushion, sweat salting her eyes and the whole pool reeling about her. A sound like the wind flapping a flag—slapping it—came and went; Brian was applauding again. She mouthed a slack smile to where she thought he was, and tried to stop quivering.

"No, it's not that easy, is it? Where on earth did I get that idea from? Del? Oh, to hell with Del. I don't need Del for this. This—this's *Cynthia's*."

After she had flat-footed across the pool and into the house, she took a tumblerful of bourbon, told herself it was water, and drank it in four choking gulps. She ran the bath, reeling over the edge, until it was scalding, all the time murmuring "Good old Cynthia, good old Cin!" With a second tumblerful of bourbon she leaned against the wall, head lolling like a doll's, and dipped in a foot. Her squeal brought Brian in from the living room.

"Can I come in too? Hey, Mom?"

"Later on. 'Stoo hot for you, honey. Now you—you go an' tidy up the house—your toys. For later. Nice and tidy now."

Brian scowled. "Hey, Mom, will Dad bring me some—"

"Not tonight. No. But you go and tidy up for him. That's a good boy." She set the glass on the flat at the rear end of the bath and lowered herself, wincing, flinching, into the water. She burned. At once she ran in some cold and swished it backward. Then, with eyes closed, she gulped again, heaving her throat up but, somehow, keeping most of the bourbon down. And she thought, like a woman a hundred miles away, "Who told me about this? Why didn't I wait? I never know the answer to anything."

One thing she held to: a sentimental image of a small, oversized silverfish-shape which she could rock in the palm of her hand. Somehow she clambered out of the bath, skimpily dried herself, made hamburgers without onion, fed Brian, smeared him with a face cloth, and got him into bed. Then she collapsed on the couch in her bathrobe, the phone still whining at her and Wagon Train, minus the sound, still on the screen.

She woke sore and hot, the hair matted on her forehead. In the bathroom, bombarded by moths as she squatted, she discovered a faint show and thrilled with guilt. For ten minutes she stared at the flaky tissue, afraid, trying to love what she saw, but not certain how to feel or what to do. "I mustn't," she whispered, "Otherwise . . . I'll have to be careful now. My God, it's hot. And I hurt, and I feel sick."

The pool filled as she lay on her back under the clouded evening sky, head down and her legs splayed wide. A small tickle of lapping cold rose above the diameter line of her legs, just where the kneecap began to bulge. Water nosed at her loins and the cotton wad, spilled her hair sideways, and at the other end of the pool, floated the rubber mouse quietly toward her. Gently she cupped her hand, as if weighing something on her palm: wondering, hoping, waiting. Then, just before the water lay level over her belly, she forced herself to a sitting position, floundered to her feet, and went dripping into the house.

She soon found it, the issue of *Life* with full-page color photographs of embryos and fetuses. She stared at the six-and-a-half-week hunchback so much larger than life, and then went into the bathroom to check. Nothing, save stains. So she took the nail scissors and clipped round the outline from the bulbous head to the curling tail, folded the clipping neatly into four, with the hunchback inward, and with tender finesse laid it centrally in an empty cold cream jar from the bathroom cabinet. Then she screwed the lid on tight.

After five days the bleeding stopped and most of the nausea had faded. Still nothing. She had clipped on the third day. "That's it," she told herself, "I broke faith. I didn't wait. I took a changeling. If I hadn't, I'd have found it, wouldn't I? I wish I was honeymoon fresh. I looked and looked. Funny! It stood me up! I had a date and it never turned up. Well, I needn't feel so guilty, then, need I? I'll manage, now I know."

Rob was promoted full colonel soon after arriving in Vietnam. His regular weekly letter became the week's event. He always enclosed a second letter, written in large capitals, for Brian. And she wrote punctually back, first her own reply, and then guiding Brian's hand for his. A pity, Rob said, about the false alarm. But no: *she* could reenter the Church; he wasn't going to. He hadn't time, anyway, not to mention inclination.

Safe and already dried into a buff-colored curl, the folded paper stays in the cold cream jar, never looked at, flanked by looking glass and jewel box, with Rob's letters to her neatly stacked behind it. Cynthia never sleeps in the afternoons now; and if she finds herself dozing or dreaming in the old way, reads the letters in chronological order. Rob sleeps little and, in his efficient, pessimistic way, has made a will. Adèle, read-justing to her husband in Toronto, no longer muses on Cyn-thia's gradual desiccation, having long ago (it seems to her), in a flush of defensive smugness, summed the whole mess up in one unuttered sentence: "Some women have no pride, no shame." The cent is still on the floor of the pool, and the water is still back to its usual depth. Brian is in school, the twig has blown away somewhere, and the pelican has not returned. If it ever does, elbowing in from the Gulf with its pale goiter, it will have to bear a living child in its beak and, to satisfy Cynthia at all, deliver it through the mesh into the pool.

5.
The Sun in Heat

"*F*rom the very first sunup I have burned after the Y-shaped cleft in her behind while she humps over like a woman intent on a stocking. Gorgeous to the core, all the way in from that surface culvert at whose lip a ruby arc-lamp seemed to blaze, she dawdled and shimmied in front of me with all the slither and jounce of a tart egging on Jack the Ripper. Ah razors, she'd clearly asked for them before! And now she was asking again.

" 'Take us,' begged her double wounds. 'We're putting out. And never mind the dusty stuff.' But I couldn't get even near the bulbous furnace of her zone, estimably several billion light years away.

"M 20 was her professional number, but I called her Trif (for Trifid), envying the phallic telescopes on Earth, especially Flagstaff and vile-named Lick, which nightly preserved her obscenest poses on cold color film. Out in the brightest sector of the Milky Way, she outshone me and mine, and no amount of overhearing terrestrial voyeurs' talk—about aperture, exposure, emission, or increase in sensitivity by a factor of four—brought her nearer or gave me a vicarious feel. There she rode, floating on her lovely buns in the vicinity of the Milk Dipper, and all I could do was incandesce, boost hydrogen into helium, blind baseball fielders as they maneuvered beneath the ball, and grow prominent (natch) under my halo of gas.

"Spotty.

"In heat.

"A merely medium, dullish star. The John Payne of galactic Hollywood. If even he.

"I'd have been better sawing pond ice in your upper Mohawk Valley.

"Needless by now to make the introductions, do the honors: but my coevals, and others, call me Sol. I've never yet tried to beat the system, never wandered off the reservation, never cooled off or gotten overheated. I'm still here, near the North American Nebula, in the Orion Arm of the galaxy called after Milk. I even know that an opening sentence ought to be: (a) surprising, (b) true, (c) beautiful, (d) rich with metaphysical heft. And it wasn't. I know, I know. I should have said something more like the following: (a) Went out; (b) Have the hots for Trif; (c) Am golden smeary cocoa brown, a fire-eater, a fireball, a regular hot-rod; and (d) Confess to immortal longings I cannot contain.

"Too bad.

"The trouble is, I'm not always capable of thinking, what with being self-blinded, more liquid than solid, a clutch of globy meniscuses, with my gases furring up around me and my red-hot vomit spurting entire parsecs into the middle distance. Across the Way. Who could concentrate when he spent most of his time in states of total physical breakdown? See the reputation I've acquired: busy, sweary, unruly, all-seeing, et cetera. A candle. An orb. The lap of Thetis. I make love move. I rise a ribbon at a time. I peak into every privy. I'm given two and a half pages in Bartlett's *Familiar Quotations*, but that's paltry considering the uncountable time I've been on the premises. No one has yet looked me in the eye and been grateful for it.

"Fee, fi, fo, fum, I boil my blood to scum.

"I'm a star of the type called G-O.

"I'm where I'm at, I suppose, only because everything's got to be some place. On the quiet I think of myself as a blood-red rhino waiting to charge.

"As to how a thing such as I can think at all, I won't even suggest; all's electric here, and every climbing spicule has a heart, is a bit of the main myself.

"At first I blazed extra fierce at my hangers-on, hoping astronomers would receive, and their space probers transmit, my valentine to Trif; but no such luck. Or, I hoped, by burning brighter than usual, I'd catch her eye, or the wet eye in her purple fundament, if that receives photonically. Yet I went unnoticed, with my starkest tics dubbed spots, my blinkings and winkings lumped together under some cold solar heading cooked up by stargazers. I ask you, how does a body get through? After billions of years of waiting, how *state*? Outsize heliograph, I wax autistic. Livid scrotum in ether, I almost got to the point of committing the first act of self-abuse in space! Imagine the golden yield of that. Yet nothing happened: I just went on performing. Business as usual. Taken for granted. I here, she there, fixed as lovers on a Grecian urn.

"Clearly, something had to give. One day, taking a deep incinerative breath, I blasted a spicule out and held the pressure as it jetted narrowly away, twisting and coiling. This in her direction. And all along that probing filament I throbbed my need, the one word 'Trif.' Such was motion, though, with me and mine helplessly being driven toward Hercules and her traipsing off to God knows where (forever in view although forever receding), the whole thing backfired.

"I realized then that one part of the Way never catches up with any other. It was mother's milk blighting me. What sustained me was ruining my life, and there I was, doomed to dawdle among a handful of pesky planets—urchins, upstarts, parasites—while the object of my celestial want skimmed away over horizons all and sundry, bound for the millstone's edge and beyond, with me and mine bringing up the rear. Forgive the image: a Freudian eclipse, of course. I even, for a while, made eyes at a planet or two (pederasty, I guess), sucked-in by Venus's reputation? Earth's pizzazz. Yet such cruisings died a natural death, and I once again attended to Trif herself, my target for every night and every day. I even, after the fashion of medieval lovers (I was here when they were there), in a mix of self-pity and masochistic hubris, began to develop a solar version of courtly love, desiderating an impossible she whom I adored for being hard to get.

"Nix I got for all such shifts. I itched something fierce. In what sleep I had, I tossed and turned, setting off dire electrical upsets throughout the system, feeling done for, a dud, an also-ran. For the ascetic's way I was not born; from the big bang I came, and to a bigger bang I'd gladly go.

"Except—that word is my life's sentence—except it all comes down to a chromosphere that's only molten sheets indurated with leonine spillage; they stiffen, then melt again, and my very seed comes flowing back into the core of me. Little or nothing escapes. All sinks back as mucus on the crust which the mad Earthlings picture in their glossy twenty-dollar books.

"I roared. I groaned. I sent out hellish signals, a body-sweat along the whole electro-magnetic spectrum, but with no result.

"Suicide? I thought of it, but up here you can't preempt the evolutionary curve: before you turn white dwarf, you have to turn red giant, but I would dearly have liked, in that batting of an eye, to become a sibilant neutron star or an invisible black hole whose oral elegy—bip, beep—no one could decipher.

"Of plea-bargaining (a shorter life but a merrier), there's none out here. I even flashed entreaties to Jupiter, old partner from the time we were a binary team, but all I heard was that old eternal chaffering of radio waves. Jupe neither knew nor cared.

"To hell with the system, I told myself. I'll rebel. But how? Very down indeed, I longed for when we were all one, during the first dense concentration, all on top of one another, before I had eyes, in the heyday of the puling protoplanets, when all was jazz, and heavenly harmony so-called was a mere guess aspawning. Before (I list my ills) conjunctivitis, hives, impetigo, a spherical scrofula akin to St. Anthony's

Fire. Prayers I said, Ur-bleats, and love-sick solar moos.

" 'Oh heaven,' I followed up, 'de-create me now. No more solitary. Grant my last flare. Put me out. After all, you fetched Adam a mate; you created binary stars by the zillion; you magnificently wived the Sun-King, the surrogate-god Ra; you backed the Aztecs. Even the speed of light isn't lonelier than I. Give me my golden apple now. I'll never ask again. Amen.'

"Some prayer. I once blew the system that is mine, and that was that. No playback, no reprieve. Only duty, as if I were a ball-less beacon somewhere in Boston: a tungsten saint; a monument to Thomas Edison or someone such. Mother of God, cried I, with miserable hilarity, Ohm is where the hertz is. There was no response, no acknowledgment, and I concluded I was a dumbbell: no doubt deaf, blind, and into the bargain brainless.

"I even sang, with fluid brio, just to keep my temperature up, a snatch that ran:

"In my sol-itude . . .
Crab nebula,
Loose open cluster,
Emission nebula,
Whatever you are,
Let me have your sister.

A waste of time. Everybody looks the other way up here, as in Manhattan. So I even sank to little pleas addressed to habitués of the solar Rialto—Galileo, Barnard, Cassini, Jeans, Eddington, Kuiper, Wheeler, Sagan—but no doubt they were all about their business, earthling-uistic every one. Believe me, I felt like the invisible man of legend.

"There was nothing for it, so I began to hum, to churn, exerting might and main to bring about a flaw in my furnace, damp me permanently down. No go. Yet, looking around me at the galaxy with my special gift for viewing it as the all-sky cameras do, I marked how it resembled a long corrugated transparent sausage, crammed with planetary nebulae, dust clouds, and diffraction halos: the peristalsis of some cosmic gut, and I loathed it. Hang around my neck. Reddish badge of my courage. No doubt of it, mankind has gained a richness of experiential content denied to electrons, and that very gain disbars them from helping. Fact is, I'm the self-stoking griddle that heats the complex that sponsors the planet that nourishes the race that ignores the agonies of the heart that Sol built.

"Get off your rump, I told myself. Be more like Van Gogh, Gauguin, Francis Bacon the Second: cut off an ear (or a prominence); light out for foreign parts and the dimension of disease; scream skyward while beheading thyself.

"I did. Self-mutilated, pseudo-absent, and trunkless (as I thought), I pretended I'd done the thing that sets you free, in your marrow, no questions asked. And came full circle, to where and as I originally was.

"Yet, in my bowels a quickening began. Some new process got under way. A pinched-in fart. A metaphor in flames. A prayer with its head in its mouth. A no choking on a yes. And the five billion years I have left before male solar menopause, or whatever, shrank in that very instant to four billion. (I'm nothing if not patient.) Inferno minus an iota. All from being perturbed, het-up, daffy. It *could* be done, no matter how slowly, and to damnation with the Hertzsprung-Russell diagram that serves as solar palmistry. I was that much closer to being a red giant, at which point my photosphere reaches the orbit of Mars, vaporizing Earth as it spirals inward to my core. By then, of course, all the naked-eye stars familiar to the modern sky-observer would have evolved into white dwarfs, Trif included, and I would have dismal prospects of yearning in my greatest heat for a shrunken, dead, yet still virginal, pixie.

"Not on your life, I told myself. I am now going to expedite history. A little pucker in the groin began it; a series of breaths deep-held fomented it; and a combusting effort of will, with my obsession mounting almost to thought-transference, topped it off. My nuclear funeral boiled wild. I shivered and quaked as the years flaked off in hundreds. I created the future, my object being of course to get to her before she irremediably cooled down, thus matching my peak to hers, my biggest bulge to her time of most copious lava. Jumping the life to come: four and a half million dwindling to four million, ever netherward, while time stood virtually still for her. How I swelled, a plummy red, engulfing M.V.E.M.J.S.U.N.P. in that order, misfunctioning a mite as I received Jupiter and Saturn, the big bites, but Uranus a midge, Neptune a minnow, Pluto a pup. A radiant fireball, cannibal and demiurge in one, I began to surge down the length of the galaxy, one eye on the Cygnus rift, with my hot breath catching her up and my heart hoping to explode not too far from where it would count. I mean: plant my supernova befittingly.

"Glory be, in that short time I was everything: a swarm, a halo, a harvest. I trespassed on elsewhen, I bypassed where. I was four suns in one, a red, a white, a blue, a yellow; I spawned and quaffed a zillion moons; a mess of turbulent plasma, I writhed like an earthworm in a skillet thirty light years across. The gallant of the galaxy, I toyed with the idea of creating bacteria. Past lovely Vega, white in hydrogen lip-gloss, I sped after her, belching star-stuff as I went, doing my damnedest not to be sucked away off course, hot-headedly rushing to my goal before I turned into a diamond one mile across and rotating thirty times a second, and then next to nothing: the smile of a Cheshire cat. Such horror stories I had heard.

"Zeroing in on her cleavage, I saw one there before me, no violet arc lamp but an embedded bloodshot eye, covering her acres with stellar tiddlers, and I could contain myself no longer. 'Cheat,' I yelled as I deliquesced for the last time, 'you didn't wait! Space-whore! Star-slut! Oisvarf!' The pair of them lapped me up; I shrank; I died. I came out of my dream-delirium.

"My cry halted short, stubbed out against the purpose of all purposes, the Cause that never yields. Back to work I went; I never left it. The system moves from here to Hercules at about twelve miles a second. Enough. "All I ask is this: when you glance past my orange chops, only spare a thought for one who, solo et cetera, mirrors consummational longings of your own. Yet, do not appropriate me too readily just because I confessed a dream. For I am pandemonium gas, your heirs' ultimate executioner, and the bane of all I survey. Love I may never know, again, but your holocaust in say another five billion years I'm guaranteed. Unalterable, I, though forever in flux. Gag on your huzzahs: I am that without which you do not even have a death. I give you this witness only to remind you how different I am, in all my giving, my non-having-ness.

"Remember how unsafe I am, and *you*. I flare up without warning, even in the spiral arms of my lactic mother. And when I yearn again, as yearn I must, pray to be beforehand dead. Beware of red. Learn to eat light. Huddle to your loved one. I am the system's monk—until the next time, when I come for you. Neither truly, not faithfully, nor sincerely, nor warmly, nor ever, am I yours. Over, but not out."

6.
Brain Cell
9,999,999,999

*H*owdy-do, April 23rd 1616. Don't answer: I never have long, am always on call, like the fire brigade, interrupted or left to my own low-keyed devices. It's dark in here, with occasional fireworks that shoot clean through me, on their way to—where I never know. One of the Many (ten billion of us: same population as Mondo Novo, Cathay, and Ind combined), I rarely can espy the One as a whole, although my stock of rumors and debris grows. I'm a nonstop gossiping *child* who amasses a collection of broken eggshells. One day I'll become a cortical pyramid—oh what dizzy heights of social climbing!—fragile but flawless uniform dove-gray; until then, I stick to my last (as they say on the outside), picking at the walls of this, you guessed it, field-gray cell. Powerful-seeming, we boast at maximum ten watts, not very bright, and my everyday experience is becoming unbearable: just *imagine* (what a tactless word to use!) ten billion souls all on top of one another in this spherical reserve, as if we were Indians. Mice go mad under such conditions, cannibal or schizophrenic, so why not ourselves? Why not I? As it is, the mob prevails; feuds and alliances, purges and *coups d'état*, happen in a millisecond, and here more than anywhere else no one is an island. The main is all. I'm always vulnerable. My property isn't mine. I'm forever quiescent or excited. I can't keep up. And even what I'm doing now—talking back or thinking counter—isn't allowed, although how punished I know not. Soon, presumably, I'll find out.

The lull continues, condition Alpha, Alf for short (whereas Meg, or Omega, is a sunburst); so I'll resume, do my best. At day's end, like a kelp forester, I often relax mentally by roaming, just as mentally of course, through the upper branches of the forests that enclose me. Creatures weird and exquisite swarm about me, jellies and reefs and vinelike streamers, quite blocking the wattlight with their tangle. I need no— sorry, there was a rush on just then. A red-hot front coursed through, which means He thought intensely while dreaming. A night-Meg prevailed, speeding me up from, oh, ten twitches per second to hundreds, nay thousands. *He* is mine host. As I was saying, I need no wings or swim-fins; I live vicariously, combing the beach of this Mind or, at whim, flying, swimming, or even cycling. Poaching's the favorite local sport; after all, some of us, at our extremities, are only two hundred angstrom units apart, which is to say we don't overlap only a bit more than we do, so it's downright impractical (not to say uncivil) to tell someone to get off your doorstep. Indeed, the smallest of us, the infant oilcan-bearers, are so tiny that it cannot be known, over a period as brief as the aforesaid millisecond, where they are. The more you know their speed, the *less* you know where they are, in fact, and the more you think you know where they are or aren't, the less you know about their speed. Very wearying if you value friendship, as I do. That sort of thing may well one day become a big discovery on the outside; in here it's commonplace. It stands to reason, I suppose; I keep saying that, but Reason's quite mythical to me, part-object of a local cult.

I've been in here, I estimate, since your Aprilian 23rd of 1564, when mine host (traditionally speaking) switched on, puling and passing all beneath him, which was the time of the Great Long Alf: much fuss, yes, but just as much repose and coma. If I'd been a creative type, it's in those years I'd have zoomed. As it is now, His demands are colossal (he even sleeps energetically), and I have hardly even time for such an avocational voluntary as this. Let him thank his lucky stars we only improve with use—why, I have several grossly overdeveloped synaptic knobs, each nearer to sister- and brother-knobs than is decent, each aswill with the notion-fluid which is to the engram what foreplay lubricants are to sperms (one of the above-ground rumors I cherish). *Think of me*, I was on the point of saying, *as an encrusted tree branch*, but I withdraw that fallacy: one of my abiding problems is comparison, into which I'm often tempted. Truth told, our—no, *my*—experience is unique; and all comparisons deform it. So I am not, although I resemble these, a tollbooth on a six-lane highway, although that is close; or the baby-carriage lurching down the Odessa steps in the movie called *Battleship Potemkin*, although that is dynamically more accurate, or, for that, the copper flange in the chest of a flashlight, although that likeness in its care for volition is almost on the ball. If these flashes-forward bewilder you, the fault is hardly mine. Mine host is forward-looking, like Leonardo da Vinci, who I wish were my uncle. Hardy mote, I exist between the fact and the hypothesis, deep in a maelstrom of millions of neuronal interactions, some of them futile, some immortal. I personally receive from one hundred neighbors, and transmit to as many more. "The neighborhood fence?" you ask. Well, if you must get metaphorical, which is no doubt understandable for a designated day in April, yes; except, in here, in the ghetto, we don't play on words; words play on us, and He on them.

That much uttered, by way of introductory (a handshake before firing), I want to record my own part, for posterity of course, in perhaps the gravest crisis mine host had, I pitching my idiom forward in the guessed-at future. Minor I may have been, like a Western Union boy in the Pentagon, but major the consequences were, as I've discovered by putting together in spare time (while He slept, as now) a trillion different intuitions filched from, or accidentally shed by, idling neighbors. See how engrammatically I speak! Believe it or not, but just remember (and here I address myself to putative peers of mine in your possession, you, April, and all Aprils to follow): I am an all-or-nothing relay; I don't always fire; I have inhibitions; I'm subject to reverberation from closed self-re-exciting chains (chains I was born in); sometimes a wad leaps through me, and a hundred thousand like me, right on to the massive bridge of pulp in the corpus callosum (locally known as the Bridge of Lies), thus activating the other hemisphere of the brain, dipping through the white matter to set up a new excitatory focus a long way off. Citizen therefore of two hemispheres, I'm worldly enough for this. And, considering all the static I'm subject to from funnybones bumped and the intemperate consumption of sack, et cetera, I merit a hearing. All of us in his knowledge, in our knowledge of Him, are secret sharers. So curb your intoxication with surfing on wavefronts as they curve and loop through a multitude of nets. And hear this:

Well into it, just past the three-hundredth line of his twenty-second play, mine host struck both gold and trouble during a summer afternoon in 1601, when the sweat of his wrist and arm dun-wetted the page on which he wrote. (Thanks to massive assists from us he composed in enormous long bursts, never blotting a line save with his arm.) In full cry he came up with, *via* us, I insist, the combo well-known as *O, that this too too*, and stopped cold. Notice the repetition often slanderously ascribed to a double-firing synapse, as the jargon of the neurologists is going to have it. My first datum, as the breaker swamped me after a whole series of fringe-captures and coalescings, was of pressure on a certain area of skin, up there beyond the periscope; then of this's interacting with wavefronts that signaled muscle-sensation and warmth. The result: something massy, tensed-smooth, and warm. Perhaps it was a sense of swollen udder on a cow, but *we* never know: integration of data occurs between wavefronts generated by the most diverse receptor-organ discharges from eye and hand, or from eye and ear, or discharges from the retina, the eye-, neck-, and body-muscles, et cetera, all set adventuring among the memory bank of already congealed engrams. Ugh. What a shambles. Pity us middlemen, do.

Nonetheless, candidate number one was *sluggish*: evoking terrestrial gastroped molluscs, or smooth soft larvae. Already mine host had leaped ahead to *flesh* (his walking is a series of recovered falls), the flesh being more of a problem to him than to us, or to me, and he began stirring up the circuitry that would dump *sluggish*'s rivals. After all, he was somewhat dazed by the heat of that unusual summer, as well as weary after three hours and twenty-two minutes of writing, and, to be candid, a bit hostile to flesh after a recent dose of the Neapolitan boneache. *Sluggish* would do, being lazy, little-human, and a whit repulsive. It would distance the flesh. *Too* tapped its foot twice while, yonder, *flesh* waited in the wings, parentheses between two worlds, one doubled, the other waiting to be turned. But then *slug* grew fat and hot, exploded into ocher carrion for the region's kites and afternoon London dogs, and waves began advancing toward me at indescribable speed on several fronts. I reproduce that plenty in the runways as best I can; after all, I'm trying to elasticize a pinpoint flash. Will you settle for a wiring-plan of the engram itself?

Artwork ms. page 59

Art labels to be used:

SLUGGISH   slug

SALLIED   SULLIED

solid   sludge

soiledness   suet

Faster than *suet* liquefied into *sludge*, the *soiledness* of *sludge* triggered (it *was* that abrupt) the metathesized form *solid*, which mine host, averse to double decompositions, at once rejected, his mind seething with how too, too often his *solid* flesh had *sallied* forth liquidly only to return home *sludge-sullied* and *sluggish*, which was the number he had first thought of.

Imagine the claustrophobia in here! Ugh-huh.

And so to bed? Did he lock *sallied* home forevermore to be? Not quite. Mine host habitually pens, in his "English" hand, his *a* with the rear loop left unclosed, and therefore he set down on this occasion, as usual, but with a sigh of relief so total it sounded as if he had expired, what looked like a *u*. Hence, *sullied* for *sallied*: no fault of mine: I inhabit an enchanted loom where millions of flashing shuttles weave a dissolving pattern, always meant to be "meaningful," though never an abiding one; a shifting harmony of subpatterns. I'm not commercial, am not in trade, am not obliged to deliver the goods. So the fault, if fault there be, lies with another part of the loom—the motoric switches no doubt—as well as with mine host's own sloven nature. Daedal anonym that I am, I serve, I witness, have no license-to-deplore. Understandably, then, I sometimes, rather shortcircuitedly-minded, wish along with Him, O, that *this* too too (   ) would as well . . .

But not often. To resume: he didn't even mumble *eureka!* (I have found it!), which specific grave idiom I received vicariously. Rather than his having found it, it had found him, found him wanting, and couldn't speak on its own behalf. Mine host wrote down his line and then forgot it, which is to say that its multiple representation in the cortex—that loaded mushroom of gray fiber .1 inch thick and 400 square inches in area which forms the deepfolded surface of our twin hemispheres—wasn't enough. I mean (it often happens) that most of my neighbor neurons lost it while I retained it (being in the minority, so to speak), whereas some that I lost others retained. You can't win them all. It's all, I reckon, a matter of spike potential, depends on how readily you respond to a single excitatory synaptic impulse, which I privately think of as having a noetic erection all the way on the graph from − 70 to + 20 millivolts. Some quicken and endure longer than others do; I mean some quicken faster and endure longer. . . . I, number 9,999,999,999 (or so I surmise), I the penultimate neuron and almost the last word am one of fortune's favored, at least when I contrast myself with vicinals in here: castrati, eunuchs-born, prem.-ejackers, hangnail-membered, not forgetting those truly impotent ones in love with the Dura Mater (the hard braincap up on high who keeps us all under) or those annulled for keeps by alcohol. Forgive me, April 23rd, 1616, I *am* addressing you, but sometimes you feel like the world at large and all of time as well; like posterity in volume.

What fidgets me most is the chance of this's being a wasted record, a fond, daft, merely mutinous thing due to erase itself around May 1616, only next month (a majority vote of seven tenths of all eligible neurons having decided this). True, I may survive through connotation, or quotation even, as if some fellow or sub-host in ages hence might approach *O.t.t.t.t.s.f.* with a cerebrality fierce enough to divine my brittle solo song behind it. Or, if not an entire sub-host or fellow, or not even a complete loom, then some eerily empathetic cell, sick of serving but lovesick, and avid to travel through time. That there will be no transplants before (or even long after) next month, I am certain; that telepathy, or the introduction into craniums of changeling dreams, will postdate my end (at least as sanctioned -ologies), I am clear. But cheep on I do, chirp-chirrup, hoping against hope that what I sense coming up here from down there isn't the beginning tremor of mine host's eviction, and thus inevitably of mine. God help us, he wakes! He burns alive! Someone tell him please: *I* am the host, *he's* the dependent one. In the beginning I was his child, but now I'm one of his many fathers. It's *his* flesh must melt, so be it, but (responsibly thinking) I'm not flesh at all; and so, when (while) he goes the full distance, achieves his corpse, thawing and resolving himself into a dew of marsh gas, *I* am the Everlasting, distilled from a billion trillion echoes. Those words, those lines, that line of lines, that sixty-five-thousand-dollar subjunctive beginning *O*, oh those are my flesh. So while the line endures, on live I. Mine ex-host redounds with re-

dundancy. I, Cell 9,999,999,999, am the ghost of Hamlet
Junior's sixteenth line (I use the quarto of 1604–5 and the
projective effort of counting up the lines almost finished
me). So long as men shall live, or eyes see, so long live I,
ghostly Sadducee. Surely one day my encomiast will come,
see behind the line to its only surviving witness, who's
survived even the line's corrupted willed-on funk.

Yet a tympany down there, preluding a thunder fit to panic
a billion cells up here in the attic, gives me pause. 'Tis more
than merely his waking up, being some trauma: either on a
vast scale the neuronal counterpart of a problem clamoring
for solution (e.g., how to start *The Tempest*, which got us
all seasick, whereas *sallied-sullied* affected just a few, mainly
me) or—catch my breath—*finis* to mine host's incessantly
weaving the spatio-temporal patterns of his beloved engrams
into those continually novel and interacting forms immor-
talized as brain's children, Mind's *Kinder*. What an ague is
here! He wakes, only to know he dies, and has to do it now.
Beaumont's gone already; Cervantes too. *Kindertotenlieder?*
Child-death-songs? No, not yet. Let me be born, out of this
womby Auschwitz. Oh, please. I penultimate an ultimatum
make: the billionth cell's a ghost. I stalk. It must be so. One
always gets away, even a Mohican. Our Will is fat and scant
of breath. Our Will was made this March. Otherwise, to be
literal, phew, sometime in August 1563. The superior man
rights the calendar. But to be born, however traditionally,
on a 23rd, and on another 23rd to have to . . . that's too
much. Alpha. Bravo. Charlie. Delta. Not this thunderous
rending. Behold: The Engrammarian at last! No Folio till
1623? Again the 23! 23 × 3. Lemmings all amelt. *Eureka!*
Choking. Black. Gray. Whi . . . Mine Host, O Mega O

7.
Short Life of
Esteban Fletcher

Someone truthful about Esteban Fletcher would be his wife, except she is no longer available. So the following is at best a mosaic of snippets that have come this infidel reporter's way, out of newspapers, the mouths of gossips, letters from home and abroad, and (he confesses it now) intuitions spawned by an empathy that almost became a disaster of the mind. A man recovers from the shock of finding he has a mind only when he learns the fear of losing it. (Memo to self, for later: emblazon walls of mental abyss with gigantic white-painted fraternity signs as found in rocky gorges all the way from Pennsylvania to New England. To keep things cheerful.)

His wife's name was Elba, but she was less an exile than an anagram for able, being competent and multilingual and, for a poet-storyteller such as Esteban Fletcher, the perfect Girl Friday. She cooked with bewildering subtleties of spices (and they both gained weight unduly); she typed immaculately, requiring erasotape only half a dozen times a year; and, sexually, she was total: a maternal, sisterly courtesan of, as he told everyone, infinitely sweet breath and sleek undemandingness. (Later on, mention her reading too, superior to his: Dutch poetry, Danish philosophy, Rumanian novels, etc. As if she were not complex enough to begin with.)

One day in question, Esteban Fletcher, neat in a dove-gray washable tropical suit, strode down the steps from the back row of tiered seats, accepted the prize envelope at center-stage, spoke a few colloquial iambics down into the microphone and, being unable to bear Manhattan in early summer, left the hall as soon as he decently could and drove with Elba to the airport, their destination Jamaica. (Explain E. F., at thirty-five, now on his way career-wise too. Did his third book of poems do it: *Solar Flare*, about which the New York Times Book Review-er, although eleven weeks late, said, "He does not refine ore into metal, but gold itself into leaf"?

Nothing else from that reviewer, Lance Melmoth—
pseudonym?—in past eighteen months, so maybe he was
canned for gushing.)

Let's say they had an uneventful flight *via* Miami and by
late evening were installed in a modest villa on a residential
estate thirty-odd miles east of Montego Bay. "Honey Pot"
was the villa's name, the estate's "Sable Sands" (the redun-
dancy of which I'm sure did not escape him). The next day,
in the car hired at the airport, they bought groceries in the
nearest village, at a tiny Chinese-run supermarket, and then
settled down to their intended regimen: he to write, she to
read, both of them to diet on proteins and water. The first
day went well. They swam and sunned and consoled each
other about forgoing bread, vegetables, fruit, and alcohol and
soon forgot the only untoward incident: Esteban's thought-
less swerve to the right, instead of left, in the face of an
oncoming car. Only the other driver's last-minute near-
acrobatic maneuver saved them. "Keep left!" Elba gasped.
"Keep on keeping left." With palpitating hands, he did, amazed
that last evening he had driven without mishap all the way
from the airport.

That first week was idyllic, then, although tempered by
cravings for something sweet. They contented themselves
with hot sauces, for, as Elba explained to him, a seared palate
is almost as good as a sugared one. Each of them thinned
down and switched to a smaller size of beach-wear presciently
brought along. There was no need of a scale. Delighting in
the calls of the glutted birds, they lived on silk-fish and red
snapper cooked by Millicent, the maid. He worked on something in prose, the principle of which was a quartered hallucination: a man dreaming he is dreaming a dream within a
dream or, as Esteban amended it, a man imagining a dream
that includes its own double. Then he realized he had shifted
from a five to a four, for waking-but-non-imagining con-
sciousness framed the first, while non-imagining conscious-
ness framed the second. Undaunted, he settled for four, first

envisioning (he invented the name at random) Thanatocles the Greek sculptor who created a statue to a god-to-come and yet, against the guess, saw the statue it should become but couldn't, which in turn imperfectly resembled the god, who in any case was indistinct. Then he scrapped Thanatocles, along with the whole idea of Chinese-box resemblances, and plumped for the Many-in-the-One: this time a Catalan storyteller and poet, being garroted in the plain sunlight of a prison courtyard, who insanely at the last thinks of the rictus at the bottom of a crabapple, which resembles (for an observer) the puckered mouth of the executioner, into whose mind Esteban disdained to go.

"What are you working on?" she asked, looking up from André Melpessier's latest *roman statique, Un Iota* (One Iota), recently published by Les Editions de l'Après-midi, and half-smiling at his trance-tight lips.

At first she seemed unanswerable, too much outside him: then she seemed unnecessary to answer, too much a figment of his meditation. Finally he said the one word, "Mirrors," which seemed to satisfy her. For his part, he asked her nothing, needing only to peer to see what she was reading. Sometimes she knitted scarves, or pegged little rugs based on biological slides of such things as the inchworm, the pancreas, or the garden snail, thus celebrating an invisible pageantry too little heeded (or so she thought). (Memo to self: she both knitted and pegged both at home and in Jamaica. Such continuity of manual habits.) But for now, mostly she read, with occasional light sighs, looking up to admire the red flowers that enclosed their patio. Like a frustrated bee. I recall now her passion for stained-glass windows, nothing ecclesiastical, just esthetic.

Meanwhile he, as the afternoon cumulus rolled in on one of the celebrated high Jamaican winds, began to lose count of the successive strata within hallucination and, fixing his eyes on the brown whirr of a hummingbird, saw ellipse upon ellipse, innumerable ellipses, concentric and eccentric, a shimmering whirl of ellipses which, by their tangled skeins of repeated and intersecting curves, brought home to him a glimpse of cosmic disarray, to which a mad art attempting the inconceivable was merely a clue. Far from that dead abbreviation which the sound of speech is, he felt his entire being hide behind his retinas, where there was no demiurge to separate light from darkness, with a single word, and no Adam ready to start naming things. Yet he chatted to his brain, saying: I am close to the Tibetan *akaishic* record, where all history happens at once. He even sensed that, here on a sultry day on the Caribbean coast, he might attune himself to the All by a relentless fusion of will and receptiveness. All was available, he told himself; all could arrive.

First his foot went dead, then his leg, then his buttocks, and, by the time his nose had begun to burn and peel, his mouth felt numb. Slowly, although less neatly than the ellipses, the All went on arriving. Barcelona viewed through telescopes on a hill overlooking that city gave way to a nineteenth-century Indiana physician, McTeague or McTarg, who observed one patient's pepsis through a hole in the abdomen kept covered with a wooden lid. A small moth trapped in the chest hair of Peter the Great of Russia replaced Orbaneja, the famous painter of Ubeda in *Don Quixote* who, when he had drawn a misshapen cockerel, wrote underneath it in Gothic letters, "This is a cockerel." Adonis growing upward from his grave under beds of asparagus accompanied the warden of Tijuana jail, who read travel brochures in his office; a sack of goats' eyes from Beirut; a letter from a famous university which, having the august names ERASMUS GALILEO VOLTAIRE GOETHE DICKENS chiseled into the wall face of the administration building, had them on its letterhead too, as if advertising members of the faculty . . .

Esteban almost fainted at the onrush of the knowable; then, with a tremendous reel, went inside to drink one of his self-imposed eight glasses of water per day. Elba joined him, so as to keep the count straight. Their fifth. And each, restored from the All, or the static, to the prosaic cool of an air-conditioned room, felt grateful: he, because he and Elba were each other's children: she, because they were each other's pets. Their philosophies matched. 1. People had children only because, bullied by the cosmos, they wanted someone to bully in return. 2. People had pets only because, too spineless to bully children, they wanted something to domineer. Afflicted by a host of undistributed middles, this harmonious mutual credo kept them together, and akin, when the rest of humanity was falling asunder, and was to have bad consequences.

"Overwhelm!" he said, out of the blue. "What a word! *Whelm*. From *kolpos*, for gulf." He thought he saw his breath frost there in the bedroom.

"Overwhelmed only when underpowered," she answered, freewheeling headily in the reprieve of that climate-free air. She wondered how many British Thermal Units cooled heaven.

Then they embraced at length, but not passionately. With five more weeks to come, they felt no obligation to be trite. Soon it rained, but they heard it only distantly, and when the rain stopped they were asleep, each (I presume where I dare not stage-manage!) anticipating the other's dreams in oneiric synch. (Memo: his sinusitis.)

Saturday, the next day, he drove carefully to the village to buy more chicken, while she resumed *One Iota*. Hours later, for the telephone system there was less a system than a toy for the taciturn, a call to the estate's main office brought news that he had driven on the right again and this time had collided with a car driven by a Jamaican. Had the other driver been American—or, for that, a European, a Chinese or even a shifting sinistral from Franz Josef Land—all might have been well; both would have gone right. As it was, he had head injuries, was already in the local hospital in Falmouth, and needed surgery. The estate manager, a disconsolate expatriate Yorkshireman called Swannick, who hated heat and was married to a Jamaican beauty, drove her. She signed. The surgeon removed a chip of bone from Esteban's right eyesocket. Swannick, a man of considerable influence, arranged a room for her at the Doctor-Bird Motel, the irony of which name she missed, well knowing it was the local name for the bird that hums. She sipped iced coffee in the fetid, flower-thick waiting room, slept there in sitting-up position, and awoke at dawn. The prognosis was good, but recovery and tests would occupy weeks. Now Swannick, reassuring her about "an accommodation" (a rebate on the villa he meant), brought some of her things to the motel, some of Esteban's to the tiny hospital. It was off-season, anyway, he told her. Cheaper. Otherwise . . . She didn't care, even though they had no vacation insurance. Things could have been much worse. When she saw Esteban he mumbled at her briefly, after which she went away to sleep in a bed. Let him be well, she urged the stewards of Creation: There is no justice, only the possible and its opposite; then let it be possible; for his sake. Nine hours she slept. After a visit to the hospital, she took her first food in twenty hours, in fact breaking her diet on half a dozen counts.

Esteban fluctuated while the bruises faded and the lacerations healed. One day he would address her coherently, even ask questions about Gunnar Orsenal's *Diary of a Nordic Lilliputian*, which she was reading in translation in the half-empty motel. But, another day, he would lapse into silence and slowly work the planes of his lower face as if devising some mute rhetoric of pain. He would have headaches, Dr. Figueroa (goatee beard, scent of snuff about him) told her, and the medications would affect him differently on different days. So she visited regularly, made no demands, lulling or enlivening herself according to his moods. Overall, he seemed to be improving. What more could she ask? And, eating emotionally, she regained the weight she had lost, whereas he, thanks to the spartan hospital fare, got thinner and thinner.

One evening, faintly amusing himself by comparisons with

Blind Pew of *Treasure Island* (although he, Esteban, could see with one eye), he seemed to witness his career amassing itself in front of him in tiles or strips: My writing. Cuban mother. English-descended father. Fletcher means arrow-maker. I am tall, dark, indifferent-looking. Quarrels with my bank-destined brother, lapdog of the Chase Manhattan. Long dead in Korea. Mother hysterical. Father, in petrified grief, never heard from again except maybe four times. Life in Mansfield, Pa., troglodytic. Univ. of Syracuse best can do. Teach, not Hispanic like Fletcher Sr. *Own* lingo. All the little mags refusing for two or three years. Then all the little mags inviting. Except *Pulse*. Wages of feeling up editor's wife on reading circuit. Then Wattershedd's review. Then Melmoth's. Spot on lung. An infinitely renewable pneumonic alibi. Me never a soldier. First saw Elba on Staten Island ferry. She Ivy League. Rich from greaseproof paper used in stacking hamburgers. A farce. If as well-read as she, what a poet then. Still no poem about mother's grave. He in Chicago, remarried. All of his letters glued in atrocity album. Next to hanged Bessarabians. Burned children. Turk soldiers bowling heads on coastal sand. I like coffee. Crème de menthe. Brazil nuts—

A tiny black fly, clapped dead, shot clean through his palms like a halved micro-bullet. Or felt so. 5 a.m.'s dark purple goosed 5.10 a.m.'s thinning azure. Or the other way around. His favorite poems by himself raced by in review. A *moustache*, he had written in a poem that was an apology to his body, is a *lip-brow*. *Both my eyes are nude.* Then the one about life's being a ball of fluff on the spout of a shaving-foam dispenser. Followed by that unfinished (to be honest, *unstarted*) one about St. Augustine in a garden in Milan, René Descartes in a hot cupboard, Blaise Pascal on the night of November 23, 1654, all busily having epiphanies like poison ivy. Recoiling from that semi-failure, he vowed at a tangent that if *Time* magazine sent him another renewal notice with a midget pencil enclosed, he would mail back to them a solid log with his initials charred into it.

Trying to summon up Elba's face, he found he could not. Instead, things he had imagined but never written down—discards—came back to haunt: a house shaped like a rhino; a girl socialist called Sharon Cheraleich; coffin-shaped doors; bees making honey in the wings of a downed B-52; Hamlet at the Dew Line; Karl Marx in the White House; St. Joan on the Great Wall of China; even an inhabitant of Nogent-sur-Seine, only 65 miles from Paris, complaining that he has to keep detonators firing all night to frighten wild boars away from his newly planted fields. *Via* him, Esteban Fletcher, but not his, these marshaled themselves in formation against the blood-screen within his shut eyes: rejected because he couldn't make of them a signature, fuse with them as he almost fused with Elba. It was as if some accusatory beachcomber were masterminding his daydreams, blaming him for not creating a better One by letting into his head a bigger fraction of the Many, so that all he had was a solar systematization where he could have had a universe. Poor Esteban Fletcher, victim of his own lost options, he yearned for some way of closing eyes within closed lids, for some nictitating membrane of the mind's eye. No such thing, though. (Memo to myself: re-read his poems; hunt down the uncollected stories; check them all for this Many-and-the-One thing.)

Worse, images began to arrive which clearly had never been his, even as idle sport, and which he did not even like. Such things as humdrum vignettes of domestic squabbles, or of political infighting at the local or county levels, and car salesmen mowing suburban lawns in neat attire designed for half-relaxing in. Now he was being succubated by some earnest lady novelist of the English Welfare School, or a cigar-chomping hack thin-disguising with verbal stucco the life and times of a Baton Rouge alderman, or a fifty-year-old assistant professor of creative writing embarking at last on his life's opus in vindication of such time-honored principles as a genuine novel's having a beginning, a middle, and an end: things which Esteban Fletcher himself relished, although never in that order.

For a while he blustered, non-vocally, dismissing the images only to find them persisting: so with a bad grace he succumbed, paying his dues to the ordinary in one special fudged-up peace offering which he voiced to himself thus: "You will meet beautiful people, make beautiful friends at the Captain's two cocktail parties and other shipboard 'get-togethers.' The bride is an amateur horsewoman, the groom a corporation lawyer. After the wedding the guests devour frozen champagne in paper cones. Port outward, starboard home, is POSH." It was the most boring thing he had ever thought, but it worked the trick. Everything pedestrian went away, but the gorgeousness of things forever after remained out of reach. He knew it was there, all right, but he could not cut it; when he got so far as to write it down, it came out wrong, drab and sapless. Epiphanies and ecstasies he couldn't lift out of their homely circumstances. Beauty he found merely composition (like synthetic leather). Aphrodite was pores and capillaries (like Miss Universe). The Pyramid of Cheops was only slabs (like a tray of ice cubes). The Grand Canal was H_2O (like steam). Rhythm, of words or music, was metrics or a notation after a clef sign; and even the magic of numbers (2 plus 2 = 2 times 2) was merely an accountant's tool. Thus the overlooked everydayness of things took its revenge.

A wiser commentator than I would point out that, having at last hit on the prose of life—its dry bread and drier protocol—he should have savored the mix, all those preposterous juxtapositions, and then advanced to re-see Infinity in a grain of, say, Düsseldorf mustard: its atoms, all alike, in their invariable, irreducible, divinely designed uniqueness. But he found the Almighty's thumbprints too inhuman, convinced himself that his passion for the All had been sentimentally choosy, and thus, by ceasing to write (and almost

to observe), fell victim to (a) the previously undivulged impersonality of things, and (b) the bland. Those parts of the
All he had formerly shunned—both the divine and the
human—muscled in on him and left him inept. Either, as he
saw it, they should not be at all, or he could not, he would
not, accommodate them. Clearly he was asking the perceived
or, failing that, the perceiver, not to be.

In vain Elba, both during and long after his stay in the
Falmouth hospital ("Foulmouth" he always said), reasoned
against so captious a self-denial, calling his attention to the
lush asymmetry of amino acids under high magnification or
the arbitrary branch-twig patterns of trees, and, on the other
hand, to the infinite tonic luxury of human voices or the lure
of faces. Nothing persuaded him, not even her creation from
that time onward of first a dozen, then a score, then the first
hundred, rugs patterned after color plates in books of microscopic art. Micrography she called it. She filled their Long
Island house with them. She read, repeatedly for a whole
year, his published poems to him, but he only laughed and
jeered. She held his hand. He asked her what it weighed. She
wept. He spoke of irrigation. All he did was eat, and grow
fat. His friends he refused to see or even converse with by
telephone. In short, he began to go downhill fast, wasting
away mentally while bloating. It sounds a facetious contrac-
tion to say he had not long to live, but the heart, I understand,
is every bit that sensitive. Immobilized, he brooded (or so I
guess) on the available's not being worth writing about, spurned
all medical aid, and stuffed himself with butter, avocados,
and cream cakes, all of which Elba, in a transposition familiar
to children (love into food), gladly procured.

Transferred to a nursing home after his first stroke (as much
a stroke of fate as anything cardiac), he lived on, but living
only as, in that lovely Long Island home, he had unwittingly
settled over the long years of refusing to settle down. A
vegetable, he, come full circle. Nonstop, to soothe him, she
bathed, shaved, and talced his still enormous bulk until, one

miserable day when she was beside herself with having him but not having him, she took him home. Esteban Fletcher, with his last thought, may have reiterated that the universe was not worth it, but she decided *he* was. Now he became more glabrous than ever, even faintly translucent like certain kinds of whipped cream. Reassuring herself that he couldn't get anything but better, and half-expecting him to retort with a formula from their first year together ("Don't be a stranger, now"), she began the labor of the ninth wedding anniversary, beginning with his back and the insides of his arms, using the finest black fiber-point, handwriting the first poem of *Solar Flare* in flawless copperplate on his left shoulder-blade.

Weeks later she absent-mindedly lathered him but then found the razor taking nothing off: even the post-mortem crop had ceased. And so, less grieving than thankful he was no longer subject to that phase of the universe's pastoral, she gave him a last and final shave, made room for the remaining poems (the whole of his first book and half of the second) and, wearing a face mask even in the air-conditioned cold of their bedroom at 30 degrees F., but also a track-suit, completed him. Then she phoned the literary editors that he was ready for review and gave him back to the universe. Safe in her asylum now, she does nothing but recite the poems and, as if impediment were her calling, answers none of my letters. So the present temporary truth about Esteban Fletcher will have to suffice, desultory parenthetical memos and all, until the whole truth can somehow be made to tell itself. I have other treasures to disinter.

8.
Brain Waves of a Stone Age Man

I

*R*otanev had been with the Alduvi for two months before they revealed to him their most secret mystery, but already he had witnessed the plumage dance, the sharpening at full moon of pencil-like sticks, and the males' chests painted white with crushed funguses.

He knew what these ceremonies meant: the plumage was the womb, the sticks were phallic, the white chests represented death. Uneasy at so readily interpreting their vivid ways, he recorded the details on tape, film, and in his spiral-bound notebook, wishing the primitive mind were not so predictable. Or even the man of Man, period.

The idiom varies, he thought, from here to Ethiopia, from the Amazon to New Guinea; but the constants, the abiding worries, loom up again and again like mesas of the soul. I just wish the Alduvi, or any tribe, would come up with something new: say, a fear that Earth will shrink to the size of a human kidney, or that trees are people who know that people are really trees. *Any*thing.

Hence his unscholarly excitement when Mn-Choka, the paunchy middle-aged chief, mentioned the Unondondo ritual. First, however, Rotanev had to be initiated. He agreed, drank the prescribed milky syrup and began to hallucinate (thinking, at one point, he saw himself burning at the stake, at another that azure eggs were cascading from his nostrils).

Then he passed out.

While he lay unconscious on a carefully arranged bed of leaves, the Alduvi covered his eyes with fast-drying clay, then sealed his orifices with a paste made from vulture fluff and the blood of an okapi. They buried him to the waist in earth and lit a ring of fires round him, chanting what he later discovered was the Immune or Enclosed Song.

Making his notes afterward, Rotanev marveled at Mn-Choka's willingness to describe and explain. The man took enormous pride in the tribe's customs. His English was awkward, but more through disuse than through deficiency; like many African chiefs he had been away to school and had spent a few uneasy years on a British campus: in Mn-Choka's case, Exeter.

"I also," Mn-Choka told him, "played the game of soccer."

When the Unondondo ritual began, Rotanev told himself he would never feel more distant from his birthplace, Cazenovia, New York, than in the next hour. Mn-Choka and two elders of fearsome aspect lifted toward the noon sun a length of tree trunk hollowed into a drum shape. They set it down reverentially. From within they took a skin bag tied with thongs, out of which Mn-Choka produced, with grave relish, a ball of black hair like a small tumbleweed; a glittering army-surplus steel mirror; and, as Rotanev held his breath, what was indubitably a book, soiled and split, but still a book.

As Mn-Choka bade him look closely, Rotanev saw the faded title on the spine, *Customs of the Alduvi and Other . . .* but he saw no more, aware that he and Mn-Choka were sharing a rite within a rite. Prompted by the chief's wily grin, he took the volume in his hands and read the bottom line of the title page: University of Edinburgh Press, 1921. All his yearning lifted clear of time, of space, even of professional pride, and he joined a tribe older than the Alduvi by far.

II

What happened with the Lgloo'na tribe of Australia was even stranger. This time Rotanev had a local interpreter along, Hucknall by name, and found himself wondering if Hucknall was passing to him everything the aborigines said. He sensed something omitted, a vacancy at the heart of the Lgloo'na's antique rituals of weather dances and fire tests. Had he hit upon a tribe whose corpus of beliefs had no core? An ethics with no theology behind it? Or were they still evolving their central myth? It was hard to believe any of these explanations.

After a stay of almost six months that included two side expeditions, one to a teeth-grinding sect eastward, another to dugong-worshippers in the north, Rotanev asked Hucknall to inquire of the Lgloo'na if indeed there was no dominant god or force in their world-picture.

A prolonged hubbub ensued, after which the tribe's magic-maker, using his legs as compasses, described in the sand two circles. He seemed profoundly nervous, caught off guard. The whole area of one he then dug up with his hammerclaw toes, moaning grievously as he did so; but the other he left intact. The first circle (*disk*, thought Rotanev) he declared good, the other bad. Then he squinnied at Rotanev through his fist, bowing low until his hand was level with his knees.

How, Rotanev asked, did the two circles or disks apply? What was their source? The sun, perhaps, or the moon? "Neither," Hucknall told him after some agitated exchanges in Lgloo'na talk. "It is something much smaller, a narrow witch who enters the body and blinds them. Perhaps a disease. Or a curse. No doubt a virus."

Rotanev persisted with his inquiry and was amazed at the expressions of fear on the faces of the Lgloo'na, usually such an intrepid lot. Why, he thought, they seem almost afraid of *me.*

After a lot of nervous pausing and shuffling, a deputation including the head-man made a simple statement through Hucknall. "Asker of questions, you have found us out. We are as dingoes."

"In what?" he said as an incongruous reek of decomposing apples came to him from the North American mainland, where he was due to start a lecture-tour in only two weeks' time.

Theft of magic, came the translated answer.

"From the sky?" He looked up, pointed at the clumped cumulus, like the debris of some giant flocculator. No, they told him, not from the sky: from Rotanev himself, the Asker of Questions.

Then what?

They jabbered away, then motioned at the boxes near his tent; but he still could not fathom what magic they had pilfered therefrom. The lighter with which he lit his pipe and which he recharged with butane capsules? No. Nor his pipe itself; he had it between his teeth.

So they showed him, unearthing (or de-sabling, he later thought) from a small dune the microscope he had not used since testing it on his arrival. Kneeling once again to peer down the tube, he tilted the mirror to catch light and made it flash like a tiny discus.

That reassured them.

Then Rotanev twisted the mirror to dull, and a wail of fear came from the intently watching Lgloo'na.

"Now the witch has entered them," Hucknall said. "When the tube goes dark, she's free. When it's bright, she's trapped inside. Her name, they claim, is Rotan. It's a case of light-phobia, an odd thing out here in the desert. If I were you, I'd let them keep the 'scope. You're on the edge of being a god. It's their holy grail."

Two days later Rotanev flew home, leaving the microscope behind, but with the dazzling image of its two-inch mirror stamped on his retinas and troubling his brain. A god had come and gone; a photon witch had stayed, with the innocent tiro, Hucknall, there to watch it thrive.

III

Five years, two books, and an honorary degree later, Rotanev vacationed with his much-neglected wife in Florida and there contracted an infection in the area of his lower spine. A birth defect in the form of a tiny skin flap had begun to fester. It was the result, his wife told him, of not washing the sand and salt out of his swimming trunks after each use. So, at the bottom of his back, what seemed a boil or a carbuncle swelled and shone. He could not bear to sit and he could hardly sleep, in spite of painkillers. In the end, the emergency doctor at the local hospital drained it, explaining that such a flaw was common and could be removed by surgery if persistently troublesome. It came, he said, from cells' being trapped during gestation, an odd thing being that, no matter where they ended up, they tended to evolve into what they had always intended to be.

Which, in Rotanev's case, was a tiny vestigial hand three millimeters by four, protruding like a flange of liver within the very groove of his rear. "Backhanded," he joked, far from sanguine.

All of a sudden, crouching there over the cold, paper-covered medical table, he felt overcome by the insolent profusion of things. It wasn't that he could be taken in by an educated African, or sire a cult in Australia, though the silly arbitrariness of both episodes had galled him for years. What upset him deep down was his suspicion, after the discovery of his tiny hand, that the entire organic ferment of Creation was every bit as arbitrary. God, he had heard, does not play dice; but in its intricate vagaries Creation did. Creation was God's die. It always would be. Three events from his own life were sufficient proof of that.

He told his wife this, but she countered, as so often, with his merely having had bad luck now and then.

"No," he persisted, "Africa and Australia proved it. The object of knowledge is not knowledge. There *is* no knowledge. There is only awareness of ignorance and intuition of need. A fraud here, a delusion there. An anthropologist with an appendage! What next?"

He began to say something else but couldn't; he knew his new deformity belonged in the gathering sum of what was preposterous amid the sane amenities of life. There was a star named Phakt. Female kangaroos could supply two different kinds of milk from different teats. The universe was smaller than many conceptions of it. Some bacteria actually thrived on a diet of radioactivity. It was not even clear what a life-form was.

"You are flailing around," his wife told him. "Seen from the wrong point of view, even sanity looks wrong." But she could not appease him. Nor did the excision, three months later, of his defect or his keeping it in a test-tube on his desk, just to remind him it was separate. While it dried up into a fish scale, he worked forlornly at a new, autobiographical book, in which he and Mn-Choka and the Lgloo'na came together under the title, *A Primitive, Myself.* Rotanev was convinced that the little nether hand would grow again, and wondering not why, but only where.

When it did, he would remove himself, mere biological test-bed that he had become, from the history of Man. There is one game of dice, he told himself, that a ham-fisted mutant always wins, and not by thought or chance. He braced himself for the onset, nestling his death in a sleek spot between his cortices, at first envisioning it as a tiny mother-of-pearl bird, but soon in possession of a gaudy flamingo, which, when the time came, would not only put paid to his tittle-tattling sum of days but would also fly off with his remains, deep into the sun, where time is slow and nature never fails.

9.
The
Glass-Bottomed
Boat

*I*t began when Toby Flankers, out in the middle of Montego Bay in his glass-bottomed boat with two tourists, all of a sudden began to stamp barefoot on one of the two panels. The glass cracked but did not break, and after a few seconds of standing there fazed by its strength, he resumed his crouch at the tiller, nothing said. The tourists said nothing either, accustomed by now to the vagaries of Jamaicans. He hadn't interfered with their view of the reef. The canopied boat had wallowed and twirled, but had not sprung a leak and was, after all, his to treat as he wanted. So they kept on peering downward, half convinced that he had staged some ingenious test of the glass in the interests of safety. For twenty minutes more, until their time was up, he crisscrossed the area while they exclaimed at bluefish and brain coral. On the way back to the beach club's jetty, he even gave them a chorus or two of "Ain't She Sweet," providing himself with rhythm from a gourd filled with seeds called a *shac shac* and prefacing each fit of song with an invitation to himself: "Take it away, man," as if he were a bandleader in front of a big audience. Baffled, the tourists kept their eyes on the glass and ignored the song. They could think of nothing else to do.

So no one heard what Toby had done, and Toby only half remembered. He had wanted to stretch his legs; that was it. His feet had been hot, so he'd cooled them in the thin leakage that always brimmed on the glass. Not in any sense had he wanted to go down, feet first; he couldn't even swim. That night he invaded a contractor's yard, helped himself to glass. He walked a mile from his shack in the village called Dinner Time to borrow a glass cutter and ate bananas on the way back, picking them almost absent-mindedly. When he'd finished the rubber-cement seal, he went to sleep right away on the beached glass-bottomed boat, crooning an old song about sugar mills.

But even if his fellow villagers or other boatmen or deck-chair attendants had found out, they would not have been surprised. Toby came from Trinidad where, the rumor went, he had been much arrested for brawling in the days before steel drums, when folk made music by thumping on the ground with bamboo poles a foot thick by five long, and thumped one another with them as well, even the police. In 1937, when these "bamboo tamboo" bands were outlawed, Toby migrated to Jamaica. A model of good behavior, he worked as houseboy, gardener, beach attendant, and tourist guide, finally saving enough for a down payment on an old glass-bottomed boat, the first of two. Only one thing seemed odd: he boasted, when drunk, of weird sorties into the local jungle, where he had been accosted by a goat-faced woman white from the navel down, otherwise black. In the steaming, bird-loud nights, he said, she had given him repeated experiences of what he called the gantry-kiss, with which Falfada (as he called her) used inhuman strength to lift him off his back with his jigger in her mouth. His listeners almost believed him when he told of mighty elongations of the organ as she whirled him round by his root, faster and faster until his head swam and his juice bursting made the straight hook bend. Which was when she let him drop. Some nights, cattle egrets from upon her shoulders flew to him as she whirled him round, and sat on his belly. Other times they flew in formation alongside him in splashy parallel, like laundry on a windy line.

• • •

Show us, they said. Take us to Falfada. We too want to go merry-go-round in the dead of night.

First he took them, two or three, to a place in Paradise Pen, but nothing happened. Then, farther afield, to the Retirement River, that expedition taking an entire night. But Falfada never showed, even though he said he had pleaded with her. They paid him, and he arrived with liquor with which they swilled away their disappointment.

"Bring us Falfada," they whined, love-sick for the sorceress. "An' them cow-bird."

"Nuther night, you bet," said Toby. "She vacationin'."

One time they dumped him in a spring, and when he clambered out he told them she was right there, in the water, awaiting them. In they plunged, crowing like cocks, palming their bodies as they went under, kneeling in the four-foot depth. But no Falfada, no gantry-kiss, no birds.

"How them bird fly in water?" It was a natural question.

"Save me," they heard. "Water all same like air. Want to, them fly in ground 'self. Fly through bluestone. Inside alligator. Round and round inside little knuckle on your hand. No egret, them Falfada own *hands*. Truth."

They thumped him hard, and for a while it was like the old days of the bamboo tamboo. He vowed to surprise them even more and invited them to his shack to watch, to sample, Falfada within four corrugated-iron walls. All they found, though, was a dead manta-ray wrapped in banana leaves with an old earthenware teapot atop the heap on the bed. Falfada in a new shape, he told them, and within weeks began claiming he had enjoyed her gantry-kisses at the end of the airport runway ("her Sunderlan' flying boat that time"), in the Montego Bay town fountain right in the middle of the main square, on which occasion she had been garbed like a big policeman. And then out on one of the Bogue Islands, where—

"Her," they cynically interrupted, "big fat mermaid?" *Octopus*, he corrected them in a restrained voice; her belly had been full of soup cans that clattered while she spun him miles out over the even water. To console them, he even presented them with Falfada teeth, feathers, a scab from her granite knee, a pellet of her droppings. His narratives bloomed. He milked her and gave them rum bottles of acrid-tasting fluid. When resting, he trimmed her teeth and horns with an old nail file, which he let them handle and sniff. One day he actually brought to a cricket match a sack in which he had a newborn kid wrapped round and round with bicycle inner tubes like beige intestines. Laughed away, he left the kid behind and they kept it, at least until the morning they found its throat cut. So *somebody* believed him, had swallowed his magic, and Toby turned his attention to tourists, regaling them with tales of Falfada but gaining only costive smiles if they even looked up from the glass beneath which the reef sprawled and curled.

To blacks he said Falfada had gone to Haiti. His nights were barren, no ordinary female having the knack of the gantry-kiss. He no longer flew. To whites he revealed her in colors even more mythic than before, elaborating her into a reef queen in whose pores lurked baby barracuda, in whose armpits groupers and sharks. A deep cleft as the reef fell away was one of her ears. Lion-tawny sand thirty feet below, speckled with black sea urchins, was part of her flank. "What about the mouth?" someone asked him, and he revealed the sea itself was that, in which they all floated.

• • •

Within weeks he had become a tourist draw. Already known as a first-rate boatman, deft and polite, he became a master of ceremonies, filling his passengers' ears with tall stories while they gaped down over the high wooden lips of the two windows in the boat's bottom. Those who heard him out in exasperated tolerance found themselves coming back for more, as if his words had sunk in deep and germinated. Word went around that Toby gave double money's worth, was a visionary raconteur (though no one used that phrase), somewhat whacky, but as a helmsman beyond compare. His boat never rocked.

Soon he bought himself a new one, had "Glass Bottom" painted on the sides and put the rest of his money in the bank. His love life improved. He habitually bought rounds of drinks at the Coconut Bar. For breakfast he drank milky coffee instead of tea and substituted eggs for melon. Instead of chicken-neck stew in the evenings he had legs and breasts. Living on in the same iron shack in Dinner Time, he bought a radio, a big Mercator map of the world, a pair of fleece-lined slippers, a cherrywood pipe and a brand-new *shac shac*. A picture of him appeared in the island newspaper, captioned "Beach Notable," and he clipped it out and glued it to the iron wall.

Only six weeks later he first stamped on the glass.

And a week after that, with four passengers aboard, he did it again, somehow driven by being too comfortable in a merely Jamaican world. All day he fantasized, but he wanted more. With both legs thrust clean through the glass, he would have gone down but for his arms across the wooden hatch. The unattended outboard ground away while the passengers observed Toby, who mouthed a silent lyric with his eyes aimed down. Sea welled up. The boat began to list. Blood flowed beneath the intact glass panel on the other side. No one spoke until a high-school teacher from Ohio staggered aft, seized the tiller and steered for the beach, two hundred yards distant.

When the badly listing boat was towed in by the Bermuda ketch *Davy Jones*, which had interrupted its afternoon cruise, the beach was lined with people. A siren started up. The police took Toby to hospital on a stretcher. Others took statements. Hauled up to a stretch of new-dumped shingle, the wounded boat sat unattended. In the end, no one preferred charges against him; in fact, none of the passengers could believe he'd done it on purpose. Toby knew better, though, telling the interrogators at his bedside, "I wanted to be down. Not over the side, man. *Through*. You go over side, you no' meet Falfada. I was obliged go through the glass." They asked him why, and he launched into a long, magical ramble about the gantry-kiss, the jungle at night, bamboo tamboo, and freshwater springs. The reef was a palace of stag-horn coral, he said. The glass-bottomed boat was a royal coach. The *shac shac* was Falfada's voice. In the end the police cautioned him but chose to believe the local lunatic had just been careless and was trying to rationalize.

• • •

When the stitches were out of his legs, Toby fixed up the boat, at considerable cost, and went back to sea. But in the first week he had only three couples by way of passengers, and these newly arrived, unacquainted with local gossip. The ticket seller at the beach club guided tourists to other glass-bottomed boats. Daylong, Toby cruised between the reef and the warning cable forty yards from the sand, chanting big-band lyrics from the forties and fifties, or calypsoes in which "Jamaica" rhymed with "make her," and rattling his gourd as if to set the seeds free. "Take it away, man," he told himself repeatedly, and took it away forthwith, mimicking the noise of trumpets and trombones with a whistler's pout. Alone, uneating, he ran through his entire repertoire, making up nothing new and not even trying to remember all the words. It was as if, he told himself, he was exhausting this world before sampling the next. Falfada awaited him while he crooned himself to death. Two big cans of gas kept him going all day, back and forth along his strip of sea.

Soon he was cruising all night, with no lamp.

All day he dozed; he almost struck a buoy.

The police fetched him in, took him home to Dinner Time, ordered him to stay put. But, after a long sleep and a hasty meal of bananas and corned beef, out he went again, this time going all the way from Cornwall Beach to the Bogue Islands and back. And he had more with him: a sack of canned goods, with an opener; a pound of tobacco; a bamboo pole thick as his thigh and as long as his leg; and enough gas for several days.

Out past the reef he chugged, farther than he had ever been, with the incongruous feeling of an ice cream vendor who finds himself afloat on his cart. A mile out, with only raucous jets for company as they banked before final approach, he began to thump the bamboo on the boat's bottom to the rhythm of old digging songs, of stone-passing games played by men seated in a ring. Thump-a-thud he went, noting he was farther out than the vultures flew. Only gulls and pelicans. Down into the depths his rhythm boomed, calling on Falfada.

"Mas Eu," he shouted low over the sea, naming the uncle, Eustace, who had brought him up in Trinidad. Then he cut the engine, moved forward to mop both glasses with rag and sponge and lit his pipe. Peering down, he nodded as the boat's idle motion brought copper-tinted sand into view, fifty feet below. Air Jamaica churned overhead. The breeze picked up. A squadron of indignant-sounding gulls cut past, reflected in the glass like knives. As a cloud went over, he saw his own face, toothless, walnut-withered, unshaven, and in that instant made up his mind.

Instead of smashing both glasses with the bamboo tamboo, and going down with the boat, he started up the engine, headed for the beach, then turned back and circled to burn up gas. He aimed for the beach again, cut the engine in five feet of water, tied the rudder, then stove in both panels. After starting the engine again, he stuck his pipe in his mouth, his *shac shac* and tobacco in the sack and eased himself overboard with the bamboo pole as the reeling boat moved away. He found bottom easily, trod on a sea urchin and waded ashore in pain, where he at once urinated on the embedded spine, soon had it out, by which time the glass-bottomed boat's canopy was level with the waves a quarter of a mile out.

Fined fifty dollars, he paid in cash with a superbly delivered smile. Illusions he had drowned with their instrument. Or so he said repeatedly in the little black and yellow tent he set up on the beach club's sand just below the restaurant patio. A large poster at the tent-flap announced, in untidy letters, "The Life and Times of Falfada and Toby Flankers in the Glass-Bottomed Boat. A Tale of Blood. Music. 50¢ J. 75¢ US." At first slow, business picked up as Toby remilked his fame, embellishing with spicy items filched from JBC radio, from fillers in the daily *Gleaner*, even from his map of the world. Like a certain movie star, he had tried to drink himself to death. He had witnessed a rape from a prison cell. He had frozen in Little America, sited on Antarctica's Ross Ice Shelf; breast-stroked from Christmas Island to Starbuck Island, both in the Pacific; sung with a swing band in Casablanca. He got a bigger tent, sat in it daubed with garish greasepaint behind an ancient windshield, with *shac shac* and tamboo, confident that no offended nature goddess could fell him now. All that stuff, he told them, he'd seen through.

All her lies. "Like I haunted, man. One Jamaican feller. Dead on both feet. Cripple-up an' not in this world." He winced. He guffawed. He half bowed.

Even after the sun has waned and the beach umbrellas have been collected up and stacked, Toby reminisces on, at least until six, when he leaves to perform on the cocktail cruise of the *Davy Jones*. No one who hears him believes in Falfada, but everyone believes in hearing him out, as if truth itself no longer mattered, but only how rich-blooded one of its opponents can be. Understudies, to whom we shall one day owe all the Falfadiana we have, drink in his words. He feels he is already living his afterlife. The lies are bigger than he, a living reef of tale, available to any and every boatman until the marauding crown-of-thorns starfish pick it clean. When a story has been swallowed, it is home and true. Fictitious planets can have real moons.

10.
The Basement of Kilimanjaro

(*Medulla Oblongata*: the nervous tissue at the bottom of the brain that controls respiration, circulation, and certain other bodily functions [*New Latin, elongated marrow*])

The sands of the Kizil Kum Desert look brown from the air, red when you are on the ground, and, presumably, black when you are underneath them in the political prisoners' quarters. Not far away is Samarkand, rebuilt by Tamerlane, four hours and fifty-five minutes by plane from Moscow, an oasis town in the fertile valley of the Zaravshan River. So much for that.

The sands of the Kizil Kum Desert are blown into the prisoners' cells, mixed with coal smoke, in order to produce chronic cases of pneumonoultramicroscopicsilicovolcano-coniosis, the miner's lung disease, the point being that, when they tell you something—such as my guide, Handy Man, does while the TU-144 slow-thunders in a bank before leveling out into the approach—they are usually trying to distract you from something else. Consider, if you will, some of Handy Man's Intourist Xeno-protocol effusions, here much abbreviated by myself:

"One: Beneath us is a special agricultural project about which nothing is known in the West; its spurious designation, actually painted in bold capitals on a concreted piece of the desert, being TAUMATAWHAKA-TANGIHANGA-KOAUAU - ATAMATEAPOKAI-WHENUAKITANA-TAHU, this being the Maori for 'the place where Tamatea, the man with the big knee who slid, climbed, and swallowed mountains, known as the Land-Eater, played on his flute to the loved one.' " Camouflage, he adds, to baffle the Samarkandians who stray in this direction when hunting wildebeest or llama.

"Two: It has no climate."

—111—

"What hasn't?"

"Oh, the project, the place it's in."

"Three: It appears on no map but can be referred to by citing the intersection of two lines, the one drawn from Ulan Bator to Taipei, the other from Seoul to Bangkok, which sets it firmly in the People's Republic of China, where of course it is not. But no matter, no one has any right to know where it is, just as no one has any right to expect that guide books should always be accurate."

So far, so obtuse. Worse follows.

"Four: American SR-71 reconnaissance jets, taking off from the Kadena Air Force Base in Okinawa and streaking across the Chinese mainland at eighty thousand feet or higher, have actually photographed it as something it is not, it therefore being regarded as a secret installation worthy of a place on the Strategic Air Command's map of imperative targets."

No surprise to me: air forces have to do *something*, after all.

"Five: What is being manufactured there is, according to informed sources, *Strch prst skrz krk*, a Czech war gas which fatally gives the victim the sensation of having an enormous finger rammed down his throat. He then vomits up most of his intestines."

"Look here," I say to Handy Man, "don't give me that Intourist shit, give me the real shit. If I'm going to see this place, whose existence appears at best to be dubious, then kindly provide me with some noncriteria to eschew judging it by, lest I commit myself to some xenophobic nonjudgment."

"Dig," he smirks. "It all depends, which is what the hanging man says to Damocles (we have universities in the U.S.S.R., whatever your counter-propaganda tells you, and our literature has wit). You must think of it in this way. Here, I'll draw it on the back of this envelope, thus attracting your attention to the address on the front, which of course is bogus. Let *i* stand for insider, *o* for outsider, you and I respectively, and *K* for the Kremlin, which is all sides. Now: first we have

i's view of *K* and *o*'s view of *K*. OK? Then we have *i*'s view of *o*'s view of *K* and, it follows quite naturally, *o*'s view of *i*'s view of *o*'s view of *K*, inevitably to be followed by what I will abbreviate as
K ---- (o --- (i --- (o --- K), which is all important, whereas what I will abbreviate as
o --- (K --- (o --- (i --- (o --- K)
is almost as unimportant as
i --- (K --- (o --- (i --- (o --- K).
Simple once you've mastered it. Another way of expressing this is as follows:
KoioK + or pms oKoioK + iKoioK = Koiok.
People expect too much, you see. Their heads flame with the names of the great enclosures of our collective culture—
Anayevo,
Ozerny,
Sel'khoz,
Lepley,
Sosnovka,
Lesnoy,
Vindrey,
Yavas,
Lesozavod,
Barashevo—
and of the diseases therein isolated—Kalnins, Sado, Galanskov, Ivanov, Ginzburg, Kapitsins, not to mention such complete recoveries as Babel and Pasternak, and such partial recoveries as Siniavsky and Solzhenitsyn—and they want to know everything, simply in order to rejoice over it. But KoioK precludes that, much as you would prevent your child from handling corrosive chemicals. There are limits. Now, as to the installation you are about to visit, bear in mind that KoioK wishes to protect you from what, in top circles, are known as Inaccuracy Generators, which means seeing something in such a way that you get a distorted idea of it. Unfortunately, our latest researches have conclusively proved

that to perceive at all is to ill-perceive, a point made, I believe, by some of your eighteenth-century philosophers. Nonetheless, KoioK, which revisionism of the highest caliber is now redrafting as K-u, meaning K unperceived, would like you to visit with us, even though, in the interests of factuality, you are to see nothing at all."

My mind boggles. I tell him so:

"I'm afraid I don't follow."

"No one ever does, it is so difficult to instill the peaks of metanoetics into the minds of the commons, if you will pardon the expression. What I have in mind is a tour, in the French sense that you will have a little stroll at the end of which, having perceived nothing, and therefore having misconstrued nothing, you will part from us on excellent terms and commend us to your own government for our prudence, recommending that they do likewise. In this way, the Unseen-by-itself #1 will be able to get on better with the Unseen-by-itself #2, neither of the Unseens having been seen by the other. This, surely, is how the myth of God has endured for so long: to be seen at all is to lose face, whereas to remain unseen is to win believers wholesale. I can see you follow. My own name, for example, Handy Man, is actually an allusion to *Homo habilis*, the earliest known man whose skull survives, who possessed the physiological capability of speech. Except, you see, in talking I say nothing at all. If I say *evitative*, I mean it both backwards and forwards, so that the sum total of what I am saying is, *evitativeevitative*. So too, when I say *interlaminations*, I mean anagramic *internationalism* as well.

"Intourist guide speak with forked tongue."

"How was that?"

"Skip it, buddy-boy. We're on the ground."

He seems to think of all the things he could say, reviews them all, then dismisses them as too arbitrary; to this monolithic mandarin of near-aphasia, utterance unutterably corrupts. So I am doubly alone, sole tenant of the palindrome that reads O, not only the same back to front as front to back, but also top to bottom, bottom to top, from that side, from this, all right I *know* it looks oval, but it's supposed to be round and to roll.

So, it seems, I have discovered the wheel. Good.

All that is above ground is a small pumping station, into which we step, and here is a tiny elevator that takes us down in the pitch black. Am persuaded to walk forward after elevator halts; hear groans of effort, smell of tallow, the heat greater than upstairs in the desert of Kizil Kum, the wall surfaces bafflingly smooth.

All this with not so much as a word.
All this with not so much——.
All this with——.
All this.

A sudden pulmonary pain I refuse to heed, my hands have been planted on something hard and smooth, not metallic but warm. I move along, we all move along, my hands brush other hands and I apologize, but no one apologizes back, and I begin to develop the notion that this thing I am feeling at is infinitely long, extends all the way to the Arctic Circle. I marvel at the firm surface, smooth as a baby's bottom or some indefatigably polished apple, and estimate its height at about six feet, for I can feel the convexity begin to curl over at about five feet. The only sounds are of shuffling feet, breath pulled in and shot out, and what I can only describe as earth-tremors, as if the ground itself were giving and settling under the thing's weight. And, as I go, in a straight line as far as I can tell, I speculate wildly about what the thing is: it has neither cavities nor protuberances, varies not a jot in texture, never sounds hollow when I clap my open palm against it, and has no vibration. On the one hand, it might be a massive pipeline containing water or oil, water for the Samarkand canal system or oil for some secret missile base—no, not oil, but rocket fuel, heavy water, it might be anything: protein-impregnated mercury, molten diamonds, white-hot lava from the bowels of some eminent volcano. On the other hand, it might be quite solid, say an underground girdle round the earth, or the U.S.S.R. at least, made of ivory or some other bone. Most of all, though, it feels organic, living, like the longest and thickest dildo in the world, something with which to pleasure the bottomless craters in the ocean floor. But, I ask myself, where is the point in that? Why the superheated secrecy, why the darkness, the palpable absence of words? It must be something of colossal ingenuity and eon-shaking force. Whoever designed it must have had some fun, mustn't he, and the prisoners who built it—assuming it *was* built— must have wondered at its purpose, presumably never having seen the thing either in part or in its entirety.

On we move, inching our way like pedestrians in some political allegory inch their way along the streets with faces to the walls, and time not so much passes as dissolves. Furtively, I lick the surface of the thing and the taste is waxy and this could just be the mother of all tallow candles, giant white obelisk horizontal beneath the red sands of the Kizil Kum, awaiting the call to action, when the lights go out all over the world and the Soviet Union has this, will light such a candle that all nations will thenceforward pay a dawn-tax. I try to bite a piece off, but there is no purchase for the teeth; they slip and skid. Stabbing with a finger is no good either, nor jabbing with the elbow nor even a powerful knee-thump. The thing is invulnerable, even to interpretation.

Where Handy Man is, I have no idea; he must be down here still, shuffling his way in company with the rest of us, his head no doubt bursting with all the things he dare not say, with his anticipation of all the questions I cannot even put to him, and with the latest authorized version of Unseen-by-itself #1:

"*Kak vy pazhevyetye?*" Clumsy Russian for "How're yuh doin'?"

Unseen-by-itself #1 has no pronoun, having no noun.
Well then: Hi!
Is unaddressable.
But nonetheless addresses?
Nothing but silence, into which I now shout as loud as I can:
  "Trotsky!"
An unkempt-feeling hand squeezes itself against my mouth, one of the prisoners to be sure; the hand moves off, and all this time we have not paused, the distance traveled being possibly by now a hundred yards. Well, this is one way of walking to the Aral Sea, northwest of here, or to Tashkent and Samarkand, to the south, the neighboring desert to the west, the Kara-Kum, or to the Muyun-Kum, to the east. No matter, the thing no doubt bends at some point and restores us to the foot of the shaft, where I will be none the wiser, not even better informed. Trouble is, the human mind resists like madness the unverifiable object, is ill-equipped to accept the thing-in-itself; uneasy with quasars, dung-beetles, and quartz, gets to work to fit them into systems, and it's to the system we've invented that we respond. Oh, Purpose, thy maw is gross, thy tentacles never quit, thy policies come at a low premium.

You think I was breaking down? Am? It's true. Handy Man is better at self-stifling than I, has rigors implanted in his brain such as I have never dreamed of, enzymes that restrict the amount of chemical transmitters available and help him to clam up. I, on the other hand, leap to interpretation like a bridegroom into the chamber; have already, let me confess it, summed up this giant underground proliferation as a giant squash, edible vegetable marrow, elongated against famine, analogous perhaps with the longest bread ever baked, sixty-six feet and one inch, by J. T. Gould in Ohakune, New Zealand, or the 34,591-pound cheese made by the Wisconsin Cheese Foundation in 1964, or the three-thousand-foot sausage concocted by thirty butchers in Scunthorpe, England.

Thus the busy mind at its most pragmatic. That this thing, which I haven't even seen, can be useless, simply something to torment political prisoners with (and Cartesian-minded tourists), seems an intolerable idea, quite contrary to *nous*. I may have just encountered the first centrally-heated edible squash in human history; for all I know it may have buses running through its interior, glorious heraldic designs on its flanks, a *Cucurbitan* anthem all to itself fudged up by Dimitri Shostakovich, a symphony for squash and troglodytes. I don't care. I tread sideways on, as before, happy to obey now I know what it is that I'm touching as I go. And when, after another fifteen minutes or so, I find myself at a ladder, and am urged to mount it, and so climb up and over and down, and begin to sidestep on the return journey, I rejoice, having arrived at a positive conclusion in the absence of all, or almost all, evidence, and knowing that our mind is given us to be useful to us, not to leave us in the lurch.

11.
The Season of
the Single Women

Beachboy they call him, behind his back, to his face: bitch-boy, biche-boy, bush-boy, bshba, baba. Either way Nelson Churchill answers, which means he fits the label, lets the label fit, and he responds, at least shows the word can activate him. And all through the season of the single women, August–October, he does what a beachboy is supposed to do: no more, no less, not even when the excitements of the season fetch his Carib appetites up high, and not even when boredom on top of fatigue makes him want to go sulk in his shack half a mile inland from the suave commotion of the beach and the Hotel Cobalt.

Out of season he fiercely sows the field of his mind, each year rereading with decreasing difficulty his hardcover English translation of *Mein Kampf* filched from the lending library in Kingston, as well as *The Thoughts of Chairman Mao*, a flimsy paperback found in a deck chair near the open-air bar of the hotel. Studying Hitler, the loser, he seeks weaknesses to run down in Mao, whom he thinks a prospective winner. A third book, equally favorite, is Benjamin Franklin's *Poor Richard's Almanac*, a gift from Mrs. Cowdenbeath, the most generous (and most discerning) of the single women with whom he deals. She smiles when he quotes "God helps them that help themselves," and tells him to practice self-help whenever he can, which he does, not valuing what he gives and giving only because he's a beachboy biding his time before the bloodbath fills.

Beachboyishly grinning, he's forever thinking about the first of the mass executions he'll stage right there on the pink-white sands of the Hotel Cobalt's beach, the shallow mass grave scooped out with a bulldozer stolen from the bauxite mill a few miles away, the loudspeakers pounding the doomed with his own specially written Execution Calypso, and his aides in white-and-gold uniforms swigging rum punch from silver yacht club tankards while casually firing their carbines from the hip with the other hand. Of social reforms he hasn't thought, his main passion being to clear the land, empty the hotels and the villas, assemble a sufficient corps of blacks to justify his title of Admiral (he by now having enough oral Spanish to mark the look-at, marvel-at element in the word itself: *mira!* Ad-mira!-l). His mother was never quite sure who his father was, and such too he would make the nominal fate of the white—mainly American or Canadian—sun-hunters, of the white owners and residents, even of the eminent black novelist retired back to his native land from the fogs of London after receiving an OBE from the queen. He would like them all, just before the bullets mangle them, to arrive at anonymity through fright. And if he forgets anybody on his own version of the Day of the Long Knives, they'll pay for it by being hanged, drawn, and quartered when he remembers. That's traditional, he tells himself (whoever he is), their hearts plucked out and held aloft for the good ole Jamaican sun to tan.

All the same, he is courteous. As he's now telling Mrs. Cowdenbeath from the sand where he squats like a retainer beside her aluminum chaise longue, he has studied at first hand the manners of whites during a summer session at the university college, during which he dismayed the phoneticians with an ad-libbed dialect he claimed was spoken by a fast-dwindling Rastafarian sect up in the northwest of the island. She says nothing, and on he goes. A two-man team sponsored by the college found no trace of such words, or even such sounds, in that region, and on its return reinterrogated Nelson Churchill, who by that time had revised his imaginary language into something quite different. The experts gave up on him because he wasn't serious, and failed him in his end-of-term examination. After that, he just happened to not report a fire in the phonetics laboratory during a faculty celebration for a visiting member of the island cabinet. Lamenting the local shortage of dynamite, he removed himself (having no encouragement to stay in the haunts of literate men), first to one of the lavish villas in the suburbs where Cuban whores had reinstalled themselves in business, and where he served as both a practice-machine and peacekeeper. Should he, he tells her, later on execute them all or have them become the property of the state? Not averse to waste, all the same he didn't fancy annihilation of the island's natural resources, whether imported or not. With this and other problems festering in the truculence of his mind, he transferred himself to the northern coast and there, like an ebony Job, sat in a wilderness to think out his future. Except that it was a wilderness of green ferns and enameled birds, with bananas aplenty. Five days he stayed, unmissed (being jobless, familyless, without a friend to his name, and not yet wanted by single women) and primitively content, realizing he could stay there indefinitely, cooing to himself as big jets came in low over the forest in chunking blasts that didn't faze even the hummingbirds at their gyroscopic midair stations or shake the trees and the bananas more than the much-advertised offshore winds.

"A nice-sounding place," she murmurs, tilting her Universal Jungle Punch in its plastic coconut. "Alla that," Nelson uncouthly blurts, his mind wholly on his telling.

And now, telling her the same story all over again during her second visit to the island, he has reached exactly that point, and she is all patience, having nothing else to do. Besides, now they are more intimate than they were, although still collusive strangers. Up, he resumes, was the blue of the bluing the fat black mammas dunked into their zinc washtubs to whiten what the sun couldn't bleach. Down, that was the ants, busy as soldiers, lizards that froze or ran, and olive-green moss. Everything else was trees and steaming heat against both of which he felt he could lean. All those bananas left a film on his teeth like soap only more sweet, and he always woke with a crick in his back, the ground, if anything, too soft; but he swanned his way through the identical days, and on one of them told himself he was finally born: not on the last day he later decided, but maybe the middle one when there were fewer jets than usual. And he stayed on to let his new self relish the site of its birth.

On his return to human habitation he cut his hair an imperfect short with a long strip of glass, bloodying his scalp in the act. Scavenging on the beach, he found two compatible boots encrusted with salt and algae, and then, with money earned by motor-mowing an entire sports arena, bought a pair of blue coveralls in order to offer himself as a mechanic at the resort's most run-down garage. But, laughed away because he looked like a giant sea urchin walking on two blue laundry bags, and the boots looked no more like boots than like kettles or conches, he ran halfway back up the hill in tears, mouthing improvised neo-Rastafarian oaths. An hour later, after having reviewed where he could and could not go according to taboos of skin and class, he made three resolutions, each depending on the others and on the season just started. He acquired a decent pair of beach shorts and a thin gold chain with a medallion, and began to parade himself on the beach near the Hotel Cobalt. He squired and sired as many single women as offered, learning from them some correct and fine-uttered English. And he read as many books as possible in order to found the Revolution when the time came and thus become the island's Land-Admiral. From that time onward he felt the sun making suction on the top of his head to make him grow taller, the sand plucking at his toes to make him stick around to be fawned on (just as he in turn fawned on the white-thighed, chuckling single women when he helped them out into the shallows), and the wind speeding him on to a gorgeous destiny.

"A good start," he recalls, lapsing almost at once into local brogue, "no' evin p'lice 'pon my trail. I wuz startin' clean."

Now, this being her third year at the Hotel Cobalt, he has

told her his story for the third time; each year it has taken him longer to tell, not so much because he's had more to tell about but because he embroiders for his captive audience. Taletelling has become part of his duties, but to Mrs. Cowdenbeath only. Already an institution, he makes beach dates for the following year and accepts the gift-wrapped colognes, watches, gold-plated brushes, bird-of-paradise shirts and ties, with diplomatic gravity. Most of the stuff he sells off cheap in shantytowns in the beach's hinterland, all but the colognes, which he needs for the season, when, in the humid fug of his shack, he drenches his body with them after washing off the salt and his own musk in the rigged-up lean-to shower.

Told he's just too much, "nearly too hard to take," he smirks impersonally and tells whichever of the single women it is that his motto is "I Serve," which he has learned somewhere is the motto of a British regiment. Cavalry almost certainly, he thinks. The shack always amazes them, crude as it is on the outside and almost camouflaged with branches, some stuck into the ground, some tossed onto the roof. It has no windows but it does have a concrete door befitting a bunker, and this he's set into a solid log that turns between two wooden bearings that cup it at each end. The concrete he stole and poured himself, and the wooden parts he axed out in a day. A perfect fit, the door has to be lifted as well as pushed, which none of the women can do, and so—whatever he decides to do to them once they are inside—they can never escape him. But what amazes most is not so much his gleaming collection of stolen tools (saws, planes, chisels, mallets, and gouges), nor his library on ramshackle shelves made from crates and barrel staves (so some lines of books curve up, some down), and not even the walls solidly collaged from *Life* and *Time*, or the handmade triple bed with its quilt made from the flags of a dozen nations and the buff satin sheets that he actually bought in one of the gift shops; it is the iron trunk in which he keeps a reserve of pharmaceutical supplies in transparent plastic bags alongside jars of Vaseline as big as goldfish bowls and full of wan-looking lard. There are hot-water bottles, a couple of car aerials, several bottles of antiseptic, some lengths of ship's rope, a well-thumbed "blue" album which Nelson bought from an Egyptian mining expert in a Kingston brothel, and last, but noway least, a mint stack of towels. It is this that hones amazement into delight; each woman in her turn sees how worldly he is, how he'll succor her through every trial, every routine misadventure, and has even made provision against hemorrhage, which he'll blot both-handed like a Nubian bearing a snowdrift in his arms, all this between their swim together and her chilled vichyssoise alone at the Hotel Cobalt. Blood is on his mind, in many ways.

But Mrs. Cowdenbeath is accustomed to all of this; *doyenne* of his single women, she knows about the others and closes her mind against them.

"Good days," he tells her, "I'm free. Then there's the vexatious days when it's pay. And all the technique you got. *Where* you from again? Oh, yes." Widow of a light-plane manufacturer in Indiana, she used to go to the Virgin Islands until too many of her friends began showing up too; she smiles coldly when he says it. "All the best India you got. But mos' days I'm free, mam, and any token of your appreciation in the fullness of time . . ." He's learned from English tourists how not to end sentences, and then those vocal dots bulge and bloom in the other's mind and come home to him as dry goods minor and major inscribed NC, to be sold later by the light of paraffin lamps to sniggering villagers who regard him only in part as Land-Admiral and prefer to see him as a legal bandit: Nelzun de Screw, whose pistol is his pomaded pizzle. Or as a show-off ripe for plucking.

"Going cheap," he tells them on more than one occasion, all of his correct English having lapsed. "Silva back brushes. Brush both-two sides yuh hayd the same wun time."

They chatter at him, yellow teeth ocher in the amber light.

"Lokka, bristle to bristle," he says, and mates the brushes.

One of them motions him to make the brushes jig-a-jig, and he does that, as if making the brush-unit breathe in and out, leering his best and whispering the price thick-spittled into the faces next him. "On'y wunce ev' use', and dat to part de hayuz on a fine-fan ladee, as Gud-Abuv's my bread-cart fulla witness." But no one buys on this occasion, although they start drunkenly brushing one another's hair, the men the women's, the women the men's, and suddenly one superabundantly buxom, fruit-gnawing girl called Drydock Nellie has one brush up her pinafore, working it to a rhythm that they all begin to chant and move to, the women symbolically palming themselves and yelping like scalded birds while the men guffaw and begin to strut, and Drydock Nellie now leaps with straggly flicks of her legs behind her, down into a crouch, then up with a hysterical shriek, both hands flying now and no sign of the brush on the ground. It lasts for an hour or so until several of them stumble away to sleep, and Nelson Churchill, his mind full of Nellie, bequeaths his brushes to the village (one of his communes-to-be, after all) and strolls away into the trees.

No skin offa my nose, he tells himself. I'm brush-happy.

None of the other single women know he's the Land-Admiral-Elect of the Hotel Cobalt (his title grows in fits and starts); only Mrs. Cowdenbeath, who, as they do, calls him Nelson and who, as they are, is "mam" to him. "Services today, mam? Or do we just want to wade out and see the fishes? Cool off the lower parts of us." And some of them he picks up, *lifts*, with dexterous delicacy and bears to the water, as oblivious of black rivals (than all of whom he's a good two inches taller) as of white also-rans among the single women. This year he's booked over half his time—has, in fact, a clientele and, in some absolutely unfailing attic of his head, keeps a chart of each woman's appetite, background, and parting gifts. Mrs. Cowdenbeath, however, still comes tops: she wants to be, she's competitive and sensual. Each year, Nelson has provided her with about fifty paperback thrillers, which works out to be a couple a day, and services averaging nightly-thrice in his shack, to which he speeds her on his light motorcycle (as he does all the others, both the steadies and the irregulars). Bestriding the pillion, she has to keep reminding herself that she abolished jealousy, possessiveness—what *is* that goddamned emotion anyway?—many years ago when Cowdenbeath was stepping out on the spree that finally took him off. All Nelson knows, and cares, is that any woman who can read at that speed is entitled to whatever services she can afford. So he serves, and she counterserves with erotic tidbits gleaned from the anthropology and psychology shelves of the state university back home. Always, out of Mrs. Cowdenbeath, as it used to be said of Africa, something new—and sometimes what came out of Africa long ago. And always, too, as she departs for eleven months of planning, she gives him an ornate weapon as a gift, thus feeding his paramilitary obsessions. From his three years with her, he now has an Arabian dagger, curving and ruby-studded; a rapier like a sinuous shaft of steel light; and, most recent and his favorite, a ready-made garrote that has only to be screwed to the back of a high chair to be operational. Tempted, Nelson tested it on his own calf, winding the screw down and down, and then in and in, until he screamed sharp and sudden as he never meant to scream, and all he could think of was Adam's apples, how they must split them in the execution chair. Ggrruck.

No wonder that on the night before she leaves the island, he at last tells Mrs. Cowdenbeath straight out (as distinct from minatory hints) how he, a Rastafarian, should regard the Emperor Haile Selassie, crowned Ras Tafari, as God and demand repatriation to Ethiopia. At first she thinks he said Rotarian, but just as fast identifies Ethiopia as Abyssinia. "Better tell you de trut, mam, us Rastas dun kid aroun'. Lokka mightee funny wid hair all in a bushy tangle; dat call' de dreadlock style. One day soon dey'll be runnin' all de island and de sufferation dat goes wid it an' none uv yuh cripple-up guvvernment folks. Rastas's offal sure of their saylves."

"Then," she begins, as he oils her shoulder blades preparatory to massage; but, prone, she can't see his face, the displaced-person glaze of his eyes. So she says nothing further. For several minutes the only sounds are the spondees of his breathing as he kneads the taut muscles of her upper back and her moans of pained relief.

Now he straightens up and says, rude: "You. Wheah yuh goin' tuh run tuh then? Where all the yuhs goin' tuh run tuh then? Yuh be tellin' me that?"

Before she can answer or even comprehend what was said, he's unhooked the concrete door and stalked outside into the soft, clicking night, his face all ashake, a voice in his skull repeating "Admiral, Admiral. Three years is long enough to wait. It's time. You wait an' longer you go marry Drydock Nellie kinda trash. Now is the . . ."

Returning to the shack door, he nudges Mrs. Cowdenbeath to move back in, his muscles bulked in threat.

"You've nothing on," she softly rebukes him as she retreats. "You should—well, it doesn't really matter. No."

Ignoring that, he talks again about the Rastas, black heretics that they are, about Haile Selassie, Emperor of Ethiopia, the dreadlock style, the Land-Admiral-Elect of the Hotel Cobalt Bomb *By Appointment*—"like," he expostulates, "it sez on the liquor bottles and the jams and them boxes of fancy chocolates in the gift shops. By Appointment to the Royal Family!" And then, with accelerating fervor, he runs through the thrice-told story of his life again: the same three books he reads during the off-season, the nine months of enervating leisure, all of which she knows by heart. Again he tells her about the executions he will stage.

"You," she mocks. "And who else?"

Right back at her he blusters, "Yuh. I'm not no Land-

Admiral for nuthin'. *I got men.*"

Instead of answering she stares at him hard in the semigloom, then hitches the big white towel right around her peeling shoulders as if all-of-a-sudden modest, and dips into her purse.

"Here." Ten twenty-dollar bills. She fans them out in front of his teeth.

"Whatta that fuh?"

"To tell you the truth, you're a big, you're a beautiful black boy. Caribbean gazelle Grade A. You're good. To me. You lift and fetch and carry and kiss my hand. All the rest of it too. You give me twenty years back, which is all the years you've had, and all I do is to deduct them from forty-eight, which is *all* the years *I*'ve had. If you aren't here next year I'll be upset. Put out. But I'll survive. And, I'll tell you something else. You've got no men. You've no more gotten yourself an army than I have wings. It's time you knew something, not everything, only this. You're no Castro, you're a goddamned capitalist with a luxury dream. Take it—here. This is money, see? It's no use to me. Take it. *Nelson.*"

He can't believe it, but say it she did. "To go to Ethiopia with, to be repatriated with." He guffaws, but an awful and far-from-air-traveling scenario fills his mind and enacts itself at speed. Chairman Mao reels backward, spitted through the neck on the Arabian dagger. Hitler paws at a feebly spurting puncture in his belly and the blue-steel shaft of the rapier strikes again, unheld, passing this time through his hand and onward. Sitting erect in a barber's chair, Benjamin Franklin hmself adjusts the screw of the garrote tight against his Adam's apple and awaits the executioner's *coup de grâce*, the hand still at his throat as if cupping a broken collar together. Going, going, Nelson Churchill's brain squeaks, I'm in trouble.

"Read books," Mrs. Cowdenbeath is telling him. "*I* do. Find out things. Buy maps. Get out of yourself an—"

Nelson Churchill lets out with a strangled sound, far from guffaw, knowing no airline is going to refuse his money. To

Ethiopia he can fly; boats go there as well.

"It's for services rendered," she tells him, hushing him. "Green and portable. Now let me dress." In dumbfounded pique he has taken the fan of bills. Benjamin Franklin is still sitting, braced heroically for the end, God not helping him because he's not helping himself.

"Abyssinia." She is giggling. "A word with an abyss in it. Ah'll be seein' yah! Seriously though, penthouse politician, that's you. Why, you'd be better off in Africa, at least if you ever decided to be an amateur politician instead of a serious capitalist, which's what you damn nearly are already. You, you're a shark, and I'm a bank. I'll die rich, you see. You'll just die. Now, you want more money? It's free. On the good days, like now."

The big images in his head go small, vanish, but his last sight of Benjamin Franklin is of a bespectacled black sage in arrest motion, hand still at throat, not helping himself at all. *To what?* asks Nelson. Mao the black cherub with jowled eyes is nowhere to be seen; Hitler of the wasting cheeks, black perhaps only with fury, dwindles to a point and also goes. Nelson motions at her gifts to him—the dagger, the rapier, the garrote—still dangling from their nails against the wall. She wafts them out of existence one at a time, hand left-right, then right-left, and up-down, like a traffic cop making room for a helicopter to land in. The money is green for go, she tells him.

"OK, beachboy, I'm set." Her mind commanding her eyes to distance him as soon as they reach the lights. She's like a moviemaker proving the outsiderness of an outsider by photographing him through a window.

A kiss on his brow in the beach's penumbra is all he gets, and that's too much. Angry in tears he races the motorcycle home to the shack and bundles his three favorite books, together with as many of Mrs. Cowdenbeath's discarded thrillers as he can find, into the towel she just wore. Soused with gasoline, they all burn fast, lighting up the small clearing he cut three years before.

After that, he isn't seen on the beach for a whole week; but, sometime during an evening, in the shack with his back to the door, he sits polishing the garrote with yet another towel from his supply and humming the first lines of his Execution Calypso:

> *Mister Execution-Man, drilling holes in all them white-*
> *face animuls,*
> *Livens up de market-day—*

At a touch on his shoulder he abstractedly says "OK, mam" without turning round, and that is all. Bushy-haired and bearded, the other Rastas spring into the gloom of the shack while one tightens the wire around Nelson's throat. They take the dagger, the rapier, and the garrote, as well as the dollars, but they leave behind the dumped contents of the iron trunk. Weeks later, two local constables in soiled white shorts haul open the concrete door and find the Land-Admiral of the Hotel Cobalt Bomb By Royal Appointment burned black on the charcoal of the triple bed, with not a single fly for company, so tight the fit of the door has been.

12.
Those Pearls
His Eyes
Or, Pathologies of a Letter Unsent

*R*eread, it sounds loathsome; I just can't send his daughter something that begins, as this does, "When twin eyeballs arrived by registered mail, each resting on absorbent cotton in a pillbox, I transferred them by means of the cotton to a milkglass plate." And continues, "Then, alarmed by the reflection, I slid a sharp-edged sheet of typing paper, best bond, beneath; I do much the same with the finger-long house centipedes I spray to death in the basement, after which I tip the corpses outside on the patio. Next day they have gone, so perhaps over the years I have been infecting a tribe of chipmunks, or a chorus of cardinals, with DDT. Never mind. All of a sudden the watermark showed through like a filament, and I realized in full what I inertly knew: the eyes— those blue eyes of Manfred Vibber—were mucous, recent. And I slid the plate into the refrigerator next to the diet margarine. Incongruous, but I needed to think. In the event, I thought for several weeks.

"I am a mild man, unaccustomed to receiving eyes by mail, even from (or of) long-standing friends, and still less the eyes of other species. Notice how I refine a hypothetical distinction: mark, I'm told, of the timid. Be that as it may, I'm shortsighted too, mark (among other marks) of the Rare Book Curator, which of course I happen to be, have been these twenty years. I have written thousands of sentences, but I have collected and tended millions more, almost as if books were butterflies or birds' eggs. Except that they aren't, any more than they are eyes, although. . . . Picture, if you will, then, the astonishment when a rare book expert receives the eyes of that eminent physicist who devoted his prime to the field-ion and atom-probe microscopes, who, stranded after World War II in the Russian sector of East Germany with a wife and a young daughter to feed, survived by collecting broken marble gravestones and dissolving the marble in hydrochloric acid to make carbon dioxide, which he then piped into ammonia for a couple of hours. The resulting ammonium carbonate he dried out and packed into little bags labeled 'Dr. Vibber's Finest Baking Powder.' Bicycling round the countryside, he bartered baking powder with the farmers for flour. Bread from headstones, as he said. He got the acid from the local pharmacy, easily because it wasn't edible, and the bucketfuls of ammonia at the city gas plant. How about that, I thought, for existentialism! But none of that is news to you. Or so I suppose. 'It is good to know a little chemistry,' he said, 'even if you are a physicist.' It sounded as if he were saying it is good to have moons if you possess a planet, and I, mainly for lack of something comparably definitive to add, just told him that if the library is the heart of a university, the rare book room is the heart of the library. Where I heard that first I no longer know; I say it here only to keep from repeating the obscene thought that came as I stared at the eyes: How do *these* rate in value against the Gutenberg Bible and, oh, to be vulgar, a First Folio of Shakespeare? Worse, how to classify them? As incunabula—artifacts of an early period? As novelty bindings, along with thumb-sized dictionaries and books with vignettes painted across the gold leaf of the page edges clamped together? With Lord's-Prayer-inscribed whaleteeth, bits of wall graffitied by Lord Byron, or, hideous to contemplate, Jivaro proverbs on shrunken foreheads? No, I resolved, if anywhere these belong among those snowglobes of the Statue of Liberty or the Golden Gate Bridge, and not in a rare book collection at all. Shake them —the globes—and a little blizzard begins in the enclosed water: a pretty enough bauble. Shake these—the eyes—and who knows what mind-boggling kaleidoscope of images will start? *Kak*eidoscope! Something hideous beyond belief. No, the images were really in your father's brain, weren't they, and where is that now? Not to mention his great mind. Pardon the liberty, I beg you; how else can I say anything at all, so long after the event?

"What began his trouble, if trouble is the word, was the short leave he took during the summer: a leave from research, not from teaching, for he rarely did anything so prosaic, and this we had in common. Since his account of the events was—how shall I put it?—dispersed, laconic, and plainly inconsistent, it's hard to be certain. Such eyewitnesses (I flinch at the very word) as there were seem to have vanished or lost interest, if indeed anyone really noticed him at all. There was no doctor on board, the one appointed having been felled by a coronary only hours before sailing, which was bad luck for him, worse for your father. On board what, you may have forgotten, and with reason (my fumbling recap threatens to become bungling). It was July, and your father had bought passage on the twenty-three-thousand-ton Indonesian liner *Cusca Dam* in order to witness a total eclipse of the sun from the North Atlantic. The crassness of this so-called 'Eclipse Special' amused rather than provoked him, and he was among the first to reserve one of the eight hundred berths costing, I think, one hundred and fifty dollars for the round trip.

"'But,' I remember asking him, 'how good a view will you have? Out at sea?' The best view, I had read, would be from the north shore of the St. Lawrence River, about three hundred miles east of Quebec, at Godbout, Baie-Trinité, Il-ets-Caribou, and in the Gaspé Peninsula between Matane and Mont-Louis. I told him this, jokingly: 'My middle name is information! I'm a mine of it. I don't just buy a newspaper, I read it front to back. Which means other people don't have to. I'm a relay station for data. My essence is to be of use.' He told me, not without some of that sardonicism without which campus life would be funereal, that it wouldn't matter. He'd see enough. He had to go, since this would be the last total solar blackout within easy access of the East Coast for forty-five years, although there would be a feebler one in 1979. I let the matter drop, only incidentally marveling at his passion for—perish the phrase—eyeball witness, bizarre when you consider the panoply of instrumentation at his command, not to mention the vast resources of information retrieval. Firsthand, that's what he wanted; and now, looking back, I can see why. Each time I brush my teeth before retiring for the night, I study my physique in the mirror, touch or palp it here and there, assuring myself that all the possibilities of death are here and now within this mass. Of all known mortal options, several are latent within this bolus of bone and blubber, water and muscle (a little), which I so familiarly call Me, just awaiting in the dugout the call to action. Once thought, such a thought becomes a repetend: obligatory daily, a hundred times over, even before nightfall. So I keep busy, buying two- and three-hundred-year-old books with university funds, spending the budget like water while my own tiny cells spend me.

"Using no mind at all, as Vibber—your father—himself said, he glanced away from his rectangle of smoked glass, forgot all he knew about imperative reflectedness, and looked right into the blanked-out sun, which at once seemed to recognize him. What it was that thus distracted him, not only from his learning in such matters but also from common sense, I never learned: maybe a flying fish dazed him into some amphibian delight, or a lurch of the vessel shifted his Indonesian-American cheeseburger sideways inside him, or (which I favor) an antique hubris surged up in him and Manfred Vibber, newborn as some kind of novel trinity, became Phaethon son of Helios attempting to drive the sun chariot, Icarus initiating his own sunflare air force, and Copernicus identifying the solar middle of things. The hub of the planetary cartwheel held him and transfigured him. About which I have only this to say: a wolf in sheep's clothing is still a wolf, which is why, I suppose, a man willing to offend his own sight can inadvertently become a solar cell, anthropomorphic variety; a sheep in wolf's clothing is still a sheep, which is why none of the other passengers—oblique heli-observers all—suffered the least ill-effect. How dismal I am making it sound, whereas really it was rather glorious.

"In fact Vibber struck gold; gold struck him. And thenceforth, even while denouncing his own recklessness, he spoke as one who had parlaeyed with mc² direct and no longer needed such indirect etiquettes of cosmic polish as the C. G. Gauss medal, the H. N. Potts gold medal of the Franklin Institute, the Medard W. Welch Award of the American Vacuum Society, not even half a Nobel Prize or enough chemistry to turn headstones into baking powder. Here is how I express it:

"Net Loss: In the first instance, sight for three days.

"Net Gain: An insight into the heart of things, which I know sounds sentimental, but optimistic cosmic conjecture usually is (see my earlier profundities about the heart of a university's being the rare book room, et cetera).

"Synthesis: Everything that follows, even if, out of my incapacity to respond prudently to this retelling of a tale I have already appalled my so-called superiors with, I spin off into levity. I am such a man who, while asserting that men who repeat history aren't obliged to know any, repeatedly tries to open the door to his library vault with his Phi Beta Kappa key. Exclaims, 'Wrong key!' and so draws polemic attention to it.

"Enough of schematization. The denuded facts are that Vibber, in fact, did not receive medical attention until the ship returned to its West Side pier a day and a half later. For all that time he was blind, with a high fever. For three days and three nights, according to him, he neither saw, slept, nor ate, but remained in a hyper-conscious trance, both aboard ship and in hospital, while his visual memory staged a riot and he felt as if his eyelashes were in-turned and piercing his eyeballs at baleful speed. Then, quite without warning, the needling stopped and his sight came back (while he was on the phone to his wife, your mother I mean); but all he said to her was, 'There now, I've switched back on again. Strangely enough . . .' She, Hannah, took the last two words as the last in the sentence and sensed no points of suspension, as these things get fancily called. Relief precluded misgiving while she taxied at once from her hotel to the hospital. Soon after, she brought him home to Pittsburgh, where he prepared to spend his usual calm summer and—apart from some unprecedented outbursts of temper alternating with fits of invulnerable abstractedness—impressed her as none the worse for his mishap. Back to normal, he read the oculist's chart without error, kept his body at an exemplary 98.6 F., and experienced no headaches at all. Vibber, you might say, had come through once again.

"Or so he let people believe. One evening, over a bottle of sweet sherry in his booklined basement-laboratory (this mercifully free of centipedes), he told me a truth I could not, later, bear to recall while looking at the eyes. Ordinary vision he still had, of course, but supplemented. 'Not only,' he told me, 'am I seeing by polarized light, with all random vibrations eliminated. I'm also seeing everything in stupendous magnification. It's . . .' His explanation made me shiver: Most people with normal vision can, with a little effort, blur their sight sufficiently not to be able to decipher print that is in front of them. The eye muscles relax, fail to focus. Now, to see normally at all, Vibber had to make this same focus-blurring effort, the results of which he laughingly compared to the 'habitation-fog' of Siberia. Otherwise he saw everything vastly and perfectly, and in electromagnetic context. He even made some joke about Rent-A-Scope, but I was too preoccupied for that with how his eyes and head must feel. But no, he said: no discomfort, not even a buzz. It was like some addable harmony added. What he saw he saw with mind's eyes. Neither ECGs nor EKGs revealed anything unusual, nor did the thorough medical which the university obliged him to submit to at fifty-five, as a member of what was unamusingly called 'the presenile generation.' Only once did I doubt him, dare to think him a liar (as if living up to the sound of his name, with F replacing V), and I at once reconsidered: he was gaining nothing beyond private satisfaction; no publicity; no new discoveries; no din from space to boast about. Why the sun had brought about what it had, to him a Lutheran believer, he had no idea; but it had, as he explained, enabled him to dispense with certain instruments. He was a walking microscope that rectified its own visible light and magnified unprecedentedly. 'At will,' he said, 'once I've switched over, I can see almost anything in detail. Right now, for example, a speck of oyster shell is burning into lime which, in a drop of seawater, precipitates magnesium hydrate! Sorry to be so technical. The main difference, though, is that the speck is as big as Greenland and the drop is the size of the Pacific. I won't bore you with the process, but the end-product is magnesium. I can see it forming now.'

" '*Cui bono?*' I learnedly asked. 'What *good* is all this?'

" 'Confirmation only. Nothing I didn't know before.'

" 'Except,' I told him, 'you're doing it direct. It's as if—.'

" 'Spare me the analogy.' His face was flushed with a boyish guiltiness. 'I am just receiving a more private version of the universe. Along certain lines only. I'm far from being complete.'

"Then, perhaps piqued with being interrupted, I asked him to envision and see plain and magnify God. I think he tried to, but he couldn't: not unless, he suggested with a flicker of malice, I regarded the divinity as elegantly interiorized low-range radiant energy. So I suggested he wouldn't receive this particular subject until he himself transmitted it: to be is to be perceived, I said, but he cut me off short, again, this time with some tag from Niels Bohr—Your theory is crazy, but not crazy enough to be true. The sherry was gone. Hannah was due to arrive home (and I have always avoided her for reasons—no, I will spare you those). To sweeten parting, however, he staged an event for me, in the course of which I saw, or thought I saw, or dreamed I thought I saw, or *pretended* I dreamed I thought I saw (as if the ammonite were to enlarge its spiral into the rooster tail of the Milky Way) the town of Trenton, New Jersey, coming to a halt as it neared the New York–Pittsburgh train; my own hand inscribing in long-hand the title page of a book apparently called

Journal of the Plague Year, A.D. 1; a mile-long spermatozoon writhing up and out of Death Valley with 'EDEN' lettered in black on its flank; and what I somehow knew was the Chinese character for 'peace' being let down from the sky upon the whole of Pennsylvania, smothering it quite, except for inlets and interstices through which smoke rose until even that stopped. I tell you; it looked like revenge.

"These things having been accomplished (as Julius Caesar used to say when introducing a new phase in his account of some campaign or other), he let me stew for a while, vouchsafing no information even when, for coffee or sherry, we were alone together. He seemed to have withdrawn into extraordinariness, and I, who have never developed smooth habits of talking (although I speak in an informative staccato mainly because almost everything I say I have said before, such is the nature of my calling), had neither the heart nor the skill to sound him. The summer waxed and bulged, its pollens found me wherever I went and (as usual) made both nose and eyes seep that awful seasonal histamine, mucus, lymph, whatever it is. Only in the blue-carpeted, air-conditioned fastness of the rare book room—Caxton's Morgue, as some of its facetious and ungrateful users dub it—could I find a relief that was also social, marshaling my small platoon of quietly spoken deft females, after none of whom I hankered, as if my divorce years ago had left me numb in that appetitive region of the brain. Three or four encounters, more or less furtive, over five years, and that has been it. I am in some kind of abeyance. Understand me, Miss Vibber, were the right occasion to present itself, under the best venereal auspices, I might not dawdle; but, thus far, the overtures of certain equally divorced Mistresses of Library Science, some with a brood of offspring, have not worked the trick or met my formula. Sugar I several times tasted, like a housefly at a table bowl, and no good it did me. The body needs it not. And now my tastes are sourer, and weirder, as is evident. It helps to write these things aloud.

"How sweet-sour, then, was the day he reeled into my bookish domain, breathless, haggard, and intermittently shading his eyes, these already protected by dark sunglasses. We withdrew into my sanctum, and I ordered some tea for him, although he seemed beyond all the power of tannic acid to restore. Still, you have to do something civilly accommodating on these occasions, even if it amount only to a china cup and saucer your guest ignores. With the cassette tape-recorder from my desk before us, and switched on at his request (it like some tabloid recording angel), he began to disburden himself with ceremony or, I might say, his usual diffidence writ large. You, his daughter, were away in Europe (the University of Montpellier, was it not? Your year abroad from the Romance languages as they are done at Cornell?), and I know he was never one to confide in Hannah, whose mind, pardon the frankness, has a sedentary stance I find gruesome. My asperities, I regret to say, are those of patience shredded. Forgive me too that I refer to your late father by surname, as if he were a distant institution: he *was*, even to his friends, especially to those who couldn't bring themselves to call him Manfred. And now he has become a monument. Back to my matter, which isn't that easy to control, not least because it is for your own eventual consumption. Indulge me, please.

"It seems that, over the period end-June through mid-July, his power of magnification increased and increased. He provided me with instances (I who still marveled at the event he had somehow staged in my own mind's eye), and I think that in his position I would have gone insane. Wandering into the kitchen late at night, after Hannah had gone to bed he opened the refrigerator door and momentarily, because he was hungry, allowed his willed, normal vision to slip. The skin of a part-sliced onion burst upon him like red-hot molten iron, spotted with silver lieutenant's-bars and patches of sapphire blue. But he persisted in trying to fix a snack, refused to acknowledge the silver Cuba-shaped island in the red-cabbage purple that was the faint mold on the bread. A flake of baked potato on the rim of a plate became an acre of buff flat pebbles scattered with cherry blossom, but he spurned it, only to be dazzled by the ocher-on-black galaxy of the mustard. So as not to be engulfed by the scales of an imported Portuguese sardine, he concentrated on one scale only, but found himself staring aerially down into a steep amphitheater in which all the seats were balconies. Sugar was a cumulus ball flooded with pastel rainbows. The milk he at last settled for poured into an egg-shape that became a fringed crater with a dozen tiny moons ascending from it in a perfect ring. So he decided to drink water, but it fell from the faucet as blue-glass paperweights, triangular, hexagonal, square, and the vitamin B-12 tablet he decided his nerves required came on strong as a loose assembly of scarlet feathers and small brown spatulas. And, as was rapidly becoming clear, while everything seethed and opened up, settled and then seethed again, gaudiness was becoming almost architectural. Second to second, he lived in a visual world that had too much in it. Every slightest thing was an act of God, outclassing earthquakes and thunderclaps, and he, who of all men should have been accustomed to visions, felt 'sore afraid' (his own words, but a long way from his usual idiom).

"There were worse reasons too. The staples he tried to fit into his stapler were a vermilion ribcage. Outsqueezed toothpaste was a violet quicksand above which he floated weightlessly. Being nylon, his pajamas revealed themselves as an endlessly interlocking grid of repeated capital omegas. The flame from the Bunsen burner in his basement wriggled with two waists and three pelvises. Brass of the ashtray frothed with all colors save red. A coin's nickel was a cliff quarried deep for corpses methodically stacked. The black plastic of his pen flaked, the flake was a squadron of eastward-plunging open-beaked sienna gulls. Out of an oak splinter soared basketwork torsos with maroon breasts. Facing Hannah over the counter between kitchen and living room, he saw himself upside down on her retinas, against a network of blood vessels and one bright spot that was the optic nerve.

"Mentally he enlarged himself to stay in proportion with what he saw. His other senses began to numb out. An ability to see by X-rays came to him, and he even began to project three-dimensional laser patterns.

"Completely polarized light became only one among his awful privileges, like a stampeding of white bulls groomed into military single file, but then seen only as processing skeletons. He tried to be glad he was privy to the texture of the universe, glad about his growing powers, glad to be seeing with eyes almost divine. For a time he reveled in the purple cone-shells of DDT on the leaves in his terraced rear garden, hoping to steady himself by fixing on them and them alone, but everything else in his visual field trespassed on this devotion, scattering even the purple. And soon he felt even the unuttered language resist him, which is to say he no longer thought words (not without enormous effort) but looked volumes. Yet one word, esoteric and therefore rarely abused, he held to, as his talisman: *aliunde*, meaning 'from a source extrinsic to the matter at hand.' By this word he intended (I think) both the grotesque build-up of his eyes' power and the invasion of his view by things not even being looked at, but also Mother Nature's supplanting of his laboratory hardware. I am tempted to say that all this made him see red— there, I've said it. Of course he was angry, but he was also awed at having been singled out with only minor lobbying on his part. Of *aliunde*, really a legal term, he spoke freely, and I later came to realize it meant possession by a god: what used to be called enthusiasm. Rational as he was, he seemed also, although resentfully, to be succumbing to fervor, somewhat along these lines: Divine Design was martyring him, yet to no purpose other than the restoration of humility (something I estimate he never lost, remembering as I do the baking soda and the headstones).

"Panopsis invaded his dreams as well. Sometimes he saw,

although larger and more clearly, things he had already seen through his microscopes; but sometimes things homed in on him from the boundaries of human knowledge, attracted to him by vibration or even chance. The amino acid named glycine, for example, he already knew as resembling interlocked prisms and lozenge-shapes fringed by salmon-hued fernwork. But how, without having seen them before, did he recognize the frogspawn-textured maroon lamb chop as a section of umbilical cord, or that stunning white antlered stag, upside down against purple and royal blue, as a sliver of the human bladder? The colors, as any microscopist knows, were arbitrary, but not the shapes. Similarly, he saw a blood clot, hand-sized (or as large as Latin America, he wasn't sure), inside a fat-constricted aorta; a cross-section of Amiens Cathedral, being subjected to the pressures of gale, reproducing in its iridescence parts of the human anatomy, here a naveled belly, there two muscular legs; and, most astounding of all, a leaf-thick tree scarlet from the infrared its leaves reflected with the sun itself shining through the branches like a Christmas card star. No one principle obtained: night and day, he saw in slow motion and through time-lapse, telescopically and its reverse, by means of ions and neutrons and holographic lasers. Too much. Never, I gathered, were your father's retinas vacant. The more he told, the farther my own mind traveled in search of some counter, some principle, that would make sense of him. I thought of fishermen taking carp by archery, or with pitchforks, near the picnic tables of flooded parks. I recalled Goethe's little book about colors. I vaguely considered Glanvill's argument for Adam's having had both telescopic and microscopic vision, but dropped it as fatuous. I prefer the man who said that we see the Milky Way because it exists in our souls, not so much a flashback as a flashforward. You can see how exercised I was.

"Then I drew back, fearful of Vibber's perceptual abysses. Let him leap into the blistering bowels of his own Etna; I would meanwhile scout the rim, diligently rehearsing the current prices of certain rare books. I apologize for the seeming incivility of thus referring to your father, but it is a pain to set these matters down; I have only one view of the matter, and only one epistolary style. Not long after he left me on that confessional day in high summer (he unconsoled, I dismayed), he was discovered in the nuclear reactor building peering down into the seventy-one-thousand-gallon pool, murmuring something rhythmical at the blue glow of the Cerenkov radiation. Persuaded to leave, he vowed to return when he felt better, but to the cobalt-sixty facility next door, 'as a human sample. After all,' he said, 'the gamma rays can sterilize or cause mutations, but they don't make the sample radioactive!' I am amazed he had enough words left to say anything of the kind. Urged home finally, as you must know, he never emerged again. It was as if, at fifty-five, he died of old age, at accelerated speed, over three or four days. The pneumonia I regard as a symptom, not a cause, but what I am less certain about is the absence of anything unusual in the medical reports until, in accordance with his will (the bizarre nature of which you will appreciate), the eye hospital forwarded his 'unacceptable' eyes to me. A last thrust? A cannon-shot in dirty pool? I will never know. In the final analysis, I am grateful he remembered me at all.

"As Curator, that is. Which brings me to the arrangements I have now made. This is not the Museum of Natural History or the Rostand Institute of Biological Sciences: we are book people, and our facilities are for rare books. We dote on print. Emboldened, however, by libraries around the world that have, say, curls of the poet Shelley's hair, a piece of Arthur Rimbaud's kneecap, one of Rasputin's hands (not to mention, at one extreme, fragments of the Holy Grail, and, at the other, unmentionable anatomical relics of Napoleon), I have at long last had the eyes enclosed in perspex spheres, mounted on black velvet atop a marble plinth, and the entire artifact in a transparent refrigerator the size of a shoebox. We curators have to move with the times. This is centrally displayed in the rare book room on campus and will soon be backed by a bust now in commission. I trust you will find these dispositions suitable. We now have more visitors than ever. Sincerely yours, Virgil I. Proneskewer/Chief of Special Collections.''

Such lies I tell. Of course I cannot send it to her: it begins with, and persists intermittently in, callous impersonality as if she weren't there at all; it addresses her directly much too late; it harps on things she already knows (and which no doubt explain her renewed absence abroad); it is miserably *couched*; and I seem continually to be getting in my own way. All of this is Vibber's fault no doubt. Use it, then, for something else, such as a resignation. It is the perfect flesh out of which to carve such a thing. To hell with protocol: you do not explain resignations. When you have to go, you just go. Submit it as it is. These words, I, and Vibber's eyes, must go together, we have none of us been taken seriously, especially by the campus bureaucrats. They said their nay, but oh the eyes have it. All I hope now is that my new collection, in Boston, will have room. A new post at my age is no mere bagatelle. I pray that the faculty there doesn't sport an eclipse-visiting eunuch, otherwise . . . But the next total eclipse beyond the end of this document isn't until 2017, by which time I am certain to be in other hands, under different auspices, and no longer, by one of the deity's proxies, eyed.

13.
A Piece of
Ancient China

*W*henever he stacked pine in the kiln, Chin-Chin the former bellows-mender marveled at how fast the pine turned to ash. Not that he was unused to sudden shifts. His promotion to fireman was one, while the slurred version of his correct name, Ts'ing Ts'ing, had just as abruptly come about, although later on.

What had won him favor was his knack of fitting each broken bellows with tiny membranes of speargrass that vibrated deep inside the nozzle. A bellows became a primitive bagpipe, though less doleful in sound and less complex in effect. From then on, others made broken bellows musical while Chin-Chin tended the actual fire; menial as his job might be, it was a distinct advancement. Prowess had earned him proximity, and proximity was everything. Fire was fire, whereas air was only air.

One day, peering into the kiln, at the solid throb of the fire, he saw a blue, comb-shaped thing hover, pirouette, then come toward him as he drew back. He had no idea what it was, and it was not his way to confide in anyone. Nor would it have been wise to do so. Not long ago, the new Emperor had had all the books burned, along with musical instruments, traditional toys, and all kinds of statuary. Only what was brand new mattered, such things as, apparently, musical bellows or the unprecedented blue trim being tried out on certain plates.

Caught between the dead past and the meager present, Chin-Chin racked his brains. Was the apparition the soul of the kaolin clay, indignant at being fashioned into vulgar designs for foreign buyers? If so, it would not appear when they fired china for China. He checked when some fine-crafted ware for the home market went into the kiln, but again the comblike apparition came at him while he stayed at the visored peephole.

Only at a certain heat, he discovered, did the phantom

show. After a week he knew it showed only when china of whatever caliber sported the new blue trim, which is to say when it was not plain. Other colors could not withstand the kiln's ferocious heat, not even during the preliminary "biscuit" firing. And the blue was cobalt, mined (amid rumors) on the mountain Kao-Ling, on whose lower slopes stood the kiln and its austere chimney. Although, in its reddish-gray or gray-white form, the raw cobalt ore burned the miners' hands, Chin-Chin asked to be a miner too; but an expert fireman they could not spare; besides, such demotion would set a bad example.

So Chin-Chin went on peering and gaping until, one day, beside himself with delight and awe, he exclaimed to the overseer "The pale blue dragon comes again! Look!" Refusing to look into the kiln, the overseer reported the matter to his immediate superior, a poet who had specialized in sunsets. Had it been dawns, Chin-Chin might have fared better.

When the Emperor arrived, some days later, he watched a typical firing through the peephole and, for reasons of his own, said "I see nothing unusual. Cangue him at one. He'll unsettle everyone." Never a word about the blue phantom crossed his lips, which goes to show that emperors are masters of all they survey. If he'd seen it, did he suppress it because marvels weren't supposed to come via menials? Why then did Chin-Chin profit, however briefly, by his inadvertent invention of the bellows-pipe? No doubt the blue phantom was important, and Chin-Chin's innovation trivial. The puzzle remains. On the other hand, perhaps the Emperor genuinely saw nothing and concluded Chin-Chin was off his head. The question remains, though, of how anyone knew what Chin-Chin possibly saw; no doubt the overseer blabbed to his wife, whereas Chin-Chin was a fire-infatuated bachelor.

So Chin-Chin's neck was locked into a bisected, hinged table, with a central neckhole, for public display, as a reactionary, gagged with white fleece. After only a day, they released him, still gagged, and told him to fill the kiln with pine logs, as usual. Happily he went about his work again.

At a certain point, however, soldiers chained him to the rock floor inside the kiln itself, this time affixing a damp, plain china cangue about his neck, and resting it on the uppermost logs, which formed a roofless sentry box to shoulder height. "No china today," they told him. "Air bubbles spoil the bake." His hands were chained behind and the cangue prevented him from toppling over.

Then they fired him, hotter and hotter, and no one saw any blue, comblike apparition even when his skull glowed pink to the motley squeak of musical bellows.

When finally removed, the cangue was irregular, both warped and split, deserving to be smashed, but tinted the pale rose of a baby's gums. The Emperor had it hung next to the sealed peephole as incentive and reminder. Chin-Chin's ribcage they swung by a silken cord from a nearby tree, so that it cast a moving shadow on porcelain plates held near it, upon which nimble-fingered copyists trapped the shifting pattern in cobalt blue thinned with oil of cloves. For three reigns the blue comb in the kiln went unobserved, yet, oddly enough, the china almost always came out right; indeed, it cooked better when unspied-upon.

Thus was born the famous gridiron plate called Ts'ing Ts'ing, which is Chinese for "hello." It can only be supposed that Chin-Chin had witnessed the underground goblin known to German miners as "kobolt," notorious among them for its pale-blue mane, which shines best in undreamed-of heat, but, in the shallows of Earth, bright enough to conjure up a devil from the deep.

Among the last proverbs of that muddled bagpipe-ridden era, there is one (*kill a fact and find a truth*) which could be Chin-Chin's epitaph. Far more telling, though, is the eventual enduring fame, under gentler emperors, of the Dragon Kiln, whether the original dragon was a cobalt goblin, a twitch in the visible spectrum, or the whim of one incinerated by a dream.

14.
Occupied by
a Through Passenger

Going to that tiny apartment in a tourist town makes him far too young for what he has to do. Since he last saw her seven months ago, she has had one gall bladder attack, a fall, and a series of minor mishaps with scissors, kettle, and hot water. He has seen her through all this by phone, a vicarious paragon, but vicarious all the same. Now he is here, nothing else is allowed to go wrong, and nothing does. Yet, as soon as he goes, it starts again. If only he could stay.

One of the chains on her front door has come adrift. Not a hazard in this virtually crimefree town in Virginia, and no one bothers to fix it. She is a voluminous worrier, though, and she likes things tidy, so here he is with hammer, wrench, screwdriver, and drill, inherited from his father. Once again he braces himself for the foldaway bed on the livingroom floor, the twin mattress cushions that part in the night, the tropical heat she withers in.

This time she seems shorter, the hunch of her shoulders more pronounced, and her still-elfin face quicker into catastrophic anxiety than ever. One wrong word ages her twenty years, which is to say all the way to eight-six. First he deploys the makeshift bed, tying the strut-legs with cord pulled through holes cut into the fabric and knotted around the metal frame, then fastening the foam-rubber pads together with the same big safety pins as last time. He juggles the two-part mattress into the sleeping bag his body was supposed to fill, and spreads the top and bottom sheets while Winona, his mother, hovers about him, an abstracted rapt worshipper, tugging fabric smooth where he has left it ruffled, but too weak to tuck the corners under. She supervises, gently reminding him that before he leaves he will have to take the bed apart again, free the two halves of the mattress, remove them from the sleeping bag, and undo the cords.

Several visits ago, she first confronted him with the folding bed, having bought it from a neighbor along the hall, who also took off her hands an even smaller foldaway, which cut the price by half. Where the smaller, narrower bed had prevented him from turning in his sleep, the larger version ruined his back because, when the two halves parted company, an iron bar met his spine. At home he sleeps on a hard mattress with a solid plywood board beneath it. One accustomed to cockpits, he argues with himself, should not mind confinement. But that is just it. He loves to sprawl, tugging each knee to his chin in turn to straighten his spine. Sometimes while flying he has found his thighs and calves twitching, eager to move again, and isometrics do not help.

The room is crammed with bric-a-brac, all given her. Wherever he looks he sees does, doves, Boys Blue, milkmaids, shepherdesses, cake Eskimos, cookie jars, ornamental mugs with ornamental spoons, pitchers, ewers, fancy plates on vertical racks, dachshunds and squirrels and penguins all in glossy pot, vases by the dozen, old and current calendars, flowers mostly artificial, and a miscellany of uncoordinated clocks, several of which, buzzing or cuckoo-calling, wake him in the dead of night. Ready for all this, he dreads her aggravated frailty, each new crescendo of worry in her frown as she tunes in to something dismally invisible waiting to engulf her.

Clearly she is ready to flinch once more, doubling up into a knot of pain, then retreat to the bathroom for as many hours as necessary, purging bladder's gall and leaving behind her an almost grossly intimate bouquet of disinfectant, aviaries, and ivory teething rings. A smell not of her at all, but of her withinness, amid which he once upon a time nestled, slurping amniotic fluid. Because of a tricky heart, ever ready to palpitate, the gall bladder stays put, a time bomb of her own. Greasy she calls it. Old Greasy. She will not mind dying if only she might take him with her for company. And leave *it* behind.

How he hates to see what he calls her Mountains of Moarne expression. When a twinge comes, she sits with her hand cupped over it, mothering its heedless importunity, forgiving the threat while shifting with it into Roman matron, her face brown with agony. Then, with pain killed, she floatbabbles for two days while the off-color weals beneath her eyes grow bigger than the eyes themselves. If he tries to push a kiss or a word into that inferno, she acknowledges it with a maimed smile, a short pass of her used-up hand. "Good son," she murmurs. "You do the talking for me. I mean I want you to."

Staring at the formulaic sweetness of the half smiles on the shepherdesses, milkmaids, the boylings and the youthettes, he wishes them all a dose of porcelain colic, a hot ember in the guts, at the same time wondering to what extent their insipid rosebud mouths match feelings of hers about him, his dead father, the human race in general. Must tenderness and delicacy look so neuter, so stock? Better, he tells himself, to surround yourself with figurines of pain, gargoyles and demons, but such is not her style. He sees how all this pot embodies a love that includes him as well. His picture lurks here and there among them, as does her girlhood when she was perky, heavy-featured, with billowing pale hair so close to gray that it has never grayed, a let-off for being afflicted early on.

Does he fix the chain now, he asks. She makes him coffee while he does. In this cockpit of hers, where three steps take him right across the living room if he can find a straight path through the furniture, he feels like someone shooting elephant. The more stuff she sets against and on the walls, the smaller she seems to get. If he stretches he smashes a beak or a milkmaid's bucket. If he laughs, the pieces shake and tinkle. Yet, in another house, another home, the clutter was prodigal, the figurines were fatted, the plaster and silverboard bells that did not ring were for his each and every homecoming as student, pilot, veteran, and convalescent. The unused ashtrays were for his remains. The steins in the glass-fronted display case were for beers he'd never drink.

There is almost no room for his box of cigarillos, his wallets, his wind-up clock. He too is an exhibit in the living room. Calls himself, to himself, an inhibit too. He wonders how he looks when asleep in there, seen from above, among the sheens and smiles of her collection, upon which, at bedtime, she locks all doors, draws all drapes, formally beseeching him to tighten the faucets tight but loose enough still for her to turn. Pilots are early risers, though, so he does not bother. He tightens and loosens in one act.

While his mother sleeps, with a thermos of warm soda-water by her bed, he tiptoes about, trying to become a boy. Smaller, anyway. Now that her adoring eyes are no longer on him, he feels them all the more keenly, checking the souvenirs. Soap boxes, airline baggage labels, empty bottles of cologne, torn-off halves of theater tickets arranged by number and held in a bulldog clip. In neat ribbon-tied bundles, her birthday and Christmas cards occupy an entire drawer, telling her, that like the rest of her trophies, she has been and has been loved. She dotes on her spoor, resisting all his offers to fly her to Bermudas. The gall, she tells him. The Greasy Gall. And that is that. Her only son has used up all their luck.

He tucks her in, plants a peck on her forehead, puts out her light, and switches on the TV news, half-expecting to see her face on the screen. He turns the volume low and listens for her mild and intricate snore, marveling at how her fatless, greaseless diet has thinned her down from the buxom extrovert she once was, with gin and chicken in her hand, a kingsized smoke at the slight droop from her lip. Now, seen from certain angles, she has the lissome figure of a pre-pubescent girl, even to the nervous nibbling pluck at her lower lip, and he cannot for the life of him imagine his father or anyone tampering with her intimate anatomy, only later to make her slurp gin to wash a little Rupert out. No, the embryo holds fast. He smirks at the draft sausages laid against the foot of each door. He turns in, certain he will have a humdrum dream in the makeshift bed.

Over breakfast she asks, first, if he will please hang up his clothes, then go to the minimarket in the basement and buy a pound of sliced ham, the leanest there is. He works on the chain while she recounts catastrophes. Marjorie, her sometimes cleaning woman, has gone into hospital for treatment of a blood clot, but gangrene has set in; they have amputated both legs and part of her bottom. In the midst of all this Marjorie has had a heart attack and lain there for almost a week without a stitch on what is left of her, able only to scream when they change the dressings. And she has died. Clegg sets his mind on the chain and removes it from the bolt. Kath, an old friend in this same building, has had a stroke. She rolls unconscious under the bed, unfound for two days. Mac and Kitty have died of hiatus hernia, unable to swallow or breathe. He bores a new hole for the anchor screw while she tells him that she has the sense of being next in line, and she wonders how if you can talk about it you can't evade it.

After six deaths he loses count, he loses heart, feels more depressed and helpless than he has in years. Wanly tells her to keep up with her multi-vitamins. He will give his life to spare her the agony of the wait. He has no useful lies. He cites the longevity of her side of the family, but he half-sees the germ of her destruction intact somewhere behind her bathrobe. The food she eats feeds it, the sleep she has restores it, the care she takes of herself fortifies it. She asks him about the afterlife, and he nods the nod that says it's there if you need it. He locks the chain in place, shows her how pressure from outside the door activates the hooter provided the chain is on.

Hiatus hernia dogs him, two affronts in one. He tortures himself with how, as they sit together over snapshot albums, catalogs, the morning paper, the horror to come lurks in their company, in her safe keeping. He makes his bed while she plans his dinner with a dieter's zeal. Her life has been only an unseen accompaniment to eating and washing, breathing

and undressing. Nothing separate, precise, but only some
figment linked with her name, her face, her shape. Once the
manner of death comes into view, he thinks, much of the
guesswork goes. He almost chokes on his toast, enraged by
her resignation, stunned by her bewilderment, by her talking
sense about what makes no sense at all. Everyone's a hero,
he decides, even someone who plays second fiddle to a Cessna
Titan. Someone who, blooded by the slant-eyed enemy and
then the mountains of Abyssinia, now flies milk-run charter
flights. He wants to burn, to break out, but his mother wants
him to give up flying altogether. Then she adds that she won't
mind going if only she can take him with her. She wants
to manage this without willing his death. "Could we fly?"
Numbed, he shakes his head, half thinking that those who
have you have the right to put you down as well. He tricks
her into being the co-pilot while they sit side by side watching
a soap opera with the sound turned low. Out to Bermuda,
Grand Bahama, The Turks and Caicos they fly, low over the
translucent shallows, while he mock-indicates this or that
hotel, beach, or sound, and she warms to the make-believe,
worries about running out of fuel so far from anywhere. Or
if the winds have changed. The winds aloft, he murmurs,
and she repeats the phrase, knowing a magic formula when
she hears one. She splurges like one reborn, cooing at how
high they are flying, how little a tweak will take them far from
where they are. She knows nothing of stall or spin, mush or
yaw, but knows the loop and forbids it, and then, from the
depths of her memory, asks him about an Immleman turn,
and he says they are not a fighter plane, but a supersonic
airliner, glass-bottomed like a glass-bottomed boat. At last
he becomes the cabin steward and nests her in a pile of cushions while he, as quietly as he can, unstops the bath, the
basin, the kitchen sink, wiping up the slime and hair with
small wads of tissue paper. He makes the toilet roll holder
spin true again. And evenly. In her nap she moves tinily as
if nudging off easily frightened insects. How many days

from her last day can this one be? Not knowing, they have
to make it count. By being casual and unrestrained. With
long hugs. And nothing said. While his travel clock ticks in
its leather jerkin. He will steal away at dawn while she still
sleeps, whereas she prefers for him the different life of live-
in guardian.

Next morning, with his eyes aimed at the middle distance
behind her left shoulder, he memorizes that blank and keeps
it before him all the way to the airport. Anything but the
crumpled, blighted look that parting gives her. She has seen
the wound in the world. From the brink she has seen who
has already fallen into it.

Needing release at random, he almost finds it with an air
hostess in the airport hotel at his next stop. For two hours
they pleasure or mutedly torment each other in almost flick-
book ways, making taboo the norm until their nerves give
out. Then go their separate ways drained and faint, leaving
behind them a bottom sheet like manna for a private eye. No
one has asked me in three months he hears her saying long
afterward. I promised myself I'd say yes to the first. A Deb,
this one, but she has not asked his name or what he does, or
what has made him horny between planes. He wonders what
his mother might think and finds the thought impossible.
Before getting into bed, he calls his mother, who always
waits after he has left, then watches the electric imitation fire,
like a redhot mountain range with blackened peaks, spinning
artificial tongues of flame with little propeller wheels turning
out of sight above pieces of wavy shiny foil. He knows how
things work.

At the open window in his pajamas, he guesses how he
looks. One of the dying, taking a last look at the twentieth
century before lowering the blind, unsure if he will wake
again to raise it. Or he is an inmate of some asylum staring
out at a landscape seen by no one else, all orange feathers and
crystal trees.

In the neatly trussed springs of his mattress he hears raucous gulls. A word his father pronounces, long after death, as rawshuss. In the bray of a donkey in its field he hears the creak of an ancient door. He lives only a few hundred yards from the runway, dotes on the revolving whine, the clotted thunder spewing from the cones under the wings or below the tail. His pageantry. Back from his sad, pragmatic errand, he wonders why his mother has never worn make-up. Confidence or obtuse innocence? The same thing, he decides. His mind numbs before his eyes close. His hands clench and open on the comforter a dozen times before he drifts off, one straggler part of his mind saying make a course correction before it is too late.

Perched on the mantel, the plastic rectangle saying Occupied By A Through Passenger will remind him of his journey when he wakes. Never a filcher, he has brought it off the jet almost by accident, almost as if recognizing a phrase by Teilhard de Chardin in white on blue, with a diamond dotting the "i" in Occupied. It struck him, yes. It was one of those phrases that summed things up, or seemed to. He likes summaries of life to come from life itself and not be forced upon it from the outside. Always, he thinks, there is a better title in the book of life than in the author's head. Yet that author, stark though fuzzy, autographs from an unthinkable distance, and is just another vicariousness to whom neither hiatus hernia nor Old Greasy is more than a pawprint. If that. When he wakes he will look at the seat card, shirk its finer accidental implications, and, without daring to look, wonder if its other side is blank.

15.
In the Home Arcade, Lisle, Illinois, GOTTLIEB'S HUMPTY DUMPTY (1947)

*T*he player, an old man, whom I stealthily watch, seems to be making an urgent speech, with his thumbs pressed hard on a table in front of him, hunching forward as he makes his points, whereas of course he is playing pinball, by himself, in the funereal, echoing Home Arcade, and not one of your revved-up modern machines at all. Deep in the night.

The only lit-up thing for miles, it's *Humpty Dumpty*, a Gottlieb, Fall 1947 vintage, the first machine with flippers, and he's playing it with somber tender reverence, patient as Job, never once shoving or hudging, but with a face-softening smile (in profile at least) peering up and along the playfield, then higher at the headglass, and the whole thing is an L of amber to lemon light. *Plinkety-plinkle, ching-ching-ching*: how slowly he plays it, hardly using the flippers which were the first flippers put on a pinball game, yet scoring evenly and sedately all the same, his eyes less on the ball than on the mild mysterious yellow nymphs lit up in the backglass. Clad only in bras and panties, both zinc-ash white, they are looking mostly upward at a youth atop a crazy-paved wall almost as high as the backglass itself, and he with a red-gloved hand has ignited a bright cloud in which the words HUMPTY DUMPTY sail to the right away from him and stop short of a nonleaning tower whose terraces are unlit scores from 10,000 at the top to 70,000 at the foot. The youth has created this Milky Way of a cloud with one hand. The player has his eye on the feat. Some of the girls have pointers with which they tap on the wall, creating shadows because a light source behind them catches the full extent of the pointers, the banners, the flags; but the girls cast no shadow at all. I count six, although one of them lolls in an ornate chair at the bottom of the crazy wall, with scoreboards behind and above her, and, most extraordinary of all, right over the chair or throne, a primitive mask with white triangular mouth, one staring and one occluded eye. The floor is carpeted scarlet, and now

I see blue veils, one black body stocking. Is this a prude's pornography? Rapt as a myopic reader, the intruder is gazing at, I see it now, his own reflection in the glass, not really bothering to play save for an idle twitch of his forefingers on the flippers, but viewing his own ghost at play among the yellow nymphs, vivid in gold shirt and blue dungarees, smiling at his smile, nodding at his nod, and with his half-shut eyes pregnant as two buds in spring. In effect, the static girls enact whatever they're doing across the pale gray of his face, the white of his beard. He could be watching from two billion light years away for all the impact he has upon them, the girls and the youth, but that illusion of remoteness seems to please him as he tilts his head fractionally this way and that, watching bits of the pattern slide off the rink of his face while other bits move in. Exhaustedly joyful, he tilts mildly with each ring of the machine, each click-clack of the scoring mechanism, and he seems to be in the presence of something he's designed. I wonder if the intruder has thought of this: the *lore* of the machine. He has: the devout nostalgist at his site eats myth, and dreams too about pre-flipper times, when he shot balls with a plunger up into a bagatelle-type playfield with studs equally spaced, as in 1901. He had no more control than that. He dreads the new machines that *talk*: lisping, effete *Xenon*, which exclaims *tha!* and sighs *thelp*, *Flight 2000* with its bone-hard baritone of Mission Control (*All Systems Go, Prepare for Countdown*), *Eight-Ball De Luxe* which barks "Stop Talkin and Start Chalkin," and *Black Knight* which asks "Will you play me?" and at once, before you've had a chance to think, answers "The Black Knight Will Play *You*." Worse for him, though, are the video games, sans ball, sans plunger, sans bumpers, lite-up Specials, and multiple ball rewards; all he hears is the chuff-chuff of lasers striking in the machines of now, in the shapelessness of things to come. Enter *Xenon* he will not. Bearded Hyperion, god of sun, he begins to go down, entangled in wires. His jaws chafe. In his left hand, a red pop bumper flickers and nearly goes out. Apollo is on the way, eager to replace him and his toy; Apollo will play, not *Humpty Dumpty*, but a fazer shooting-gallery of a game called *Cosmitron, Apollygon,* or *Ionization.* Hyperion yawns and refuses to quit, just goes on doing the same thing, flipping all six flippers without overmuch concern, feeding quarters into the slot from a presumably finite supply in the pouch of his dungarees. After a while, he'll open up the machine, collect the take, and try to lose it all over again.

The playfield has seven pop bumpers, with the scores printed on top, and eight kicking rubbers, whose rubber ring stretched between two posts makes the ball rebound without necessarily scoring. "Stretched rebounds" they called them in the catalogs in olden days. The six flippers keep the ball busy, but it could be busier than the languid, doting player makes it (his mind on the myth of the machine, its historical resonance, its sedate poetry, rather than on the score). He feeds verdigris quarters into the slot, but his attention remains on the backglass, at which he stares insatiably, as if that deft consort of yellow nymphs and the cloud-creating youth atop the wall not only meant more than itself, but also took him into the unknown region past the million mark, when machines grander than *Humpty Dumpty* score you back to nought, thus making the million an invisible mental thing that only you or your spectators can provide, like an absent god, a Special that never lights up.

It might be a gaudy Rembrandt. I strain to see more detail and notice that the seated woman, at the foot of the crazy paved wall, has her legs crossed, and above the white stockings there is ginger fuzz. Is the player smiling, then, at the pubic hair on show amid an otherwise unprovoking show of bodies? Is he gently working himself off against the front of *Humpty Dumpty*, between coin chute and plunger? All the breasts are covered up, so maybe he's lapping up the one erotic touch, result of a slipped brush or a designer with a sense of humor. Scanties, yes. Thighs and hips on show, yes. But the flesh is bathed in saffron light, it doesn't look human, any more than lions' manes and the ears of chimpanzees. The glass smells of mahogany; the wood lye. The flippers are red and white, like little chips from barbers' poles. Invented by Harry Mabs, derived from the bat on the baseball machine of the 1930's, each flipper is a little tapered bat which changes pinball from a game of chance to one of skill *because you have control*: thus heralding the second dawn of free will, until existentialism shone in the third, right after World War II, when Jean-Paul Sartre and the flipper came in together, with (in '47) *Humpty Dumpty* in October, followed in December by three more: Williams' *Sunny*, Chicago Coin's *Bermuda*, and Keeney's *Cover Girl*, after which there came, all in January '48, Genco's *Triple Action*, Bally's *Melody*, and Exhibit's *Build-Up*. At first the shaft was toward the center of the playfield rather than its side—existence preceding essence, I supposed; and then they changed it round, so that your flippers moved from seven o'clock to noon, instead of from two o'clock to nine (on the right-hand side) and from five o'clock to noon instead of from ten o'clock to three (on the left). Either way, 150 degrees of movement: a fair swath out of the 360, and in *Humpty Dumpty* six times that, which is 900 degrees all told, same as coming full circle two and a half times: alive, dead; alive again and dead again; then half-alive. I seem to see him eye the ball and will it back up the board again, guiding it until it falls toward him, when it divides, and both balls go streaking up the playfield without being plungered up the runway, both of them no longer balls of steel but multicolored spheres in which tiny motes of color run awash, and the sound of the *Humpty Dumpty* is much vaster now, a medley of gongs, handbells, and Big Ben. The playfield lights up so brightly I cannot bear to look, but he stares ahead of him, as if willing the backglass to do the same, and it does, at which he rummages among the yellow-clad girls with his hands, using motions exactly appropriate to a mechanic who is adjusting the works behind the glass. Perhaps he is trying to get Humpty Dumpty (the youth on the

wall?) to come tumbling down, or he's making sure he won't.
At once the old sounds resume, the machine clinks and chimes,
the one ball in play behaves as it should while he flips the
flippers, but the figures in the backglass have changed, I can
see that. The seated woman is standing now, with a pole in
her hands aimed at Humpty Dumpty's elbows, as if to shove
him overbackward, and the other females are watching her.
The tower leans a little leftward, not enough to disturb the
patter, though, except it casts a faint shadow on the wall.

At these minor changes he seems to glow, tilting his jaw
this way and that with a look of ravished beneficence in which
pride is stronger than gentleness. "Come on in, kid," he
whispers just loud enough. "Getting old's no art, no art at
all. Come on in and try for *Humpty Dumpty*."

Without meaning to, I begin to see my life under various
pinball headings. A *biff*, an intentionally hard hit, jerks the
ball back into play just as it's on the point of going out. If
you hit a spinner that is still rotating from a previous hit, or
while another hit spinner is spinning, then you set up over-
lapping impulses which the scoring mechanism can't assimi-
late, and then you have *canceled out*. And a *captive ball* is one
that's held on the actual playfield for later use, depending on
how well you score: but of course the machine may never
let you use it. Squatted in the parcel-cluttered attic in his
mind's eye, back at home, he sighs and begins to riffle through
his catalogs again, murmuring the names of the old machines
as if inventing a catechism addressed to pain; but it no longer
cheers him to say "*Gusher, Majestic, Gypsy Queen, Dragonette,
and Sunny*," any more than the cut-rate allegory buried in
biff, canceled out, captive ball soothes me with what seems the
outline of my life.

With Alice I go questing after the White Rabbit, and with
Dorothy I go down the Yellow Brick Road, but I want no
cozy destinations, I want only the rack of birchwood and
buffed chrome, plate glass and cosmetic plastic which the
defiant, defensive, vengeful pinball machine has become, and

In the Home Arcade, Lisle, Illinois,

I no longer care to play so well, to score so high that the score reels, as we say, and the digits return to zero, when you have to start again. No, I won't turn the machine over, I'll shoot so badly I'll never score at all.

16.
Another Minotaur

*A*lmost too fatigued to notice the stench of blood and decomposing corpses on the low-lying island, the Japanese troops dug in as best they could in shell-holes that adjoined the salt mud. Threading his way between trios of inert soldiers, Lt. He-Setsu sent a four-man patrol to check if the enemy dead really were dead (and if not so to make them so). As a couple of shots rang out a hundred yards away, he nodded with world-weary neatness, sheathed his sword as if at a signal, and marveled how the blade in catching the sunset had actually seemed to slice light. In the sound of the evening tide he heard a broken *samisen*, rattling like a loose spring in a lacquered box. The nauseating air he breathed in little quanta, thinking his breaths cone-shaped. On his lips, two salts overlay the brown scum that rimmed the sunbaked skin. A reconnaissance plane with red rising sun insignia buzzed the beach and swerved left across the island. Flies made a confetti on his face as he yearned for cherry blossom or bean curd. The patrol came back, trophyless. The wind strengthened while he gnawed hard biscuit, and something, a fluid on his face, seemed to curdle and dry. He thought of a porno song he'd heard once in a night club, *I have sipped the black fluid of my mother*, but willed the refrain away. Into its play fell some gruesome sense of *déjà vu*, as if he had only an hour to live, in a scowl-eyed panic, with his neglected teeth beginning suddenly to ache. Then a low, early moon making pseudo-daylight lulled him. He flinched from his trance only a moment later, rapped out a series of orders, appointed sentries, and for the first time sat, on a hillock draped with seaweed. Five minutes' march away, a flag caught his eye; then, toward the central bulge, a lick of sunset on the ridge where observation posts had already been set up. Chilled he rubbed his pecked-looking hands together. He longed for his son, prude that the youth was, and his wife, the ever-wet, the one mincing, the other appetizingly disgraceful, with ever-hard nipples (which she pressed even against strangers while talking, like twin stethoscopes). Dragging off his cap as if tearing away a wreath, he smelled it, curled his nostrils in rebuke at the musky sweatband, and clapped the thing back on. For a while he half dreamed. A soldier brought him a small animal live, but with a shrapnel wound. It was a baby anoa, a species of small buffalo, horns just budding.

"Cook it," he ordered unthinkingly. "No. Cut it up and eat it raw." Why wasn't it yelping? He dreamed again, took *sake* from his silver hip flask, and stood erect to make water for only the second time that day.

Then he heard it, a curt aerial scuffle above the sea but not of the sea. As if an animal had scampered over. Or a very distant aircraft had dived and pulled out. It was the blood in his temples, he thought. Some trick of the humidity affecting his ears. Permafrost of the emotions cracking. It didn't come again, not for several minutes, which he timed with his filth-caked watch. Foreboding he had known, before hitting a beach or when summoned before his colonel; but this intuition of doom reminded him of something half delicious: bathing alone in hot water before returning to the university from his home town thirty miles away. At such times a desolating osmosis had made him shiver, turned his stomach into a jellyfish, and set his teeth on edge. Reverse nostalgia he called it, noting how loose a description that was. After all, despite his buried cravings for *samurai* grandeur, he was only going a short train journey to resume the study of economics. Nothing fierce. He was an A student, a fast study, a natural paraphrast of difficult books, and a lucrative career awaited him. Or it had. Now he had two decorations and a battle scar on his forearm, where a small shell fragment had skimmed through the flesh on its way to a sergeant's throat. He could still taste the sideways spurt of the other man's blood, like fluid smoke. How fared the unburied sergeant now, he wondered. The bulbous lips? The brawny trunk?

Humidity increased as night fell, quietening his men as

they squatted or half sprawled. Raw flesh for a few, combat biscuit of rice flour for most, had only made them hungrier, reviving a forgotten taste for ordinary food. Indistinctly he wanted to do more for them, have them fish in the shallows or equip them with a tub of steaming rice, but he was as tired as they. Even as the moonlight brimmed complete soon after midnight, and no attack began, he could not sleep, but peered horizontally along the beach at the sandbag forms of the men, a gleam of metal, a hand flashing pale as it rose to an insect bite and fell again. It was almost as if, along the shore of the island, broad pipes had been strewn about for placement in the earth tomorrow; all he saw was tubular, smooth angles bulging from the sand. He longed to step into the water, even if only to unstick and restick his baggy pants and short-sleeved shirt to his crawling skin. Lt. He-Setsu drifted, his mind a parasol borne by an offshore breeze through an immaculate temple garden with stone lions and bridges with concave lintels.

At the first shriek he hardly moved, musing on children at play in speckled blouses; but, as a multiple howl of mingled pain and revulsion cut the humming air, he jerked upright, dizzy and ashake. He could see nothing where the sounds came from, only a complex writhing in the gloom. An erect figure fell, leapt up again, then snapped down. Someone ran, he himself, but sprawled headlong over a body. As his gaze registered, in the moonlight that was not light, he barked a command. Now the beach seemed spread with logs or railroad timber, most of it on the move with lengthwise plunges that veered to one side or the other. Then he saw something like a lid, as of a camouflaged foxhole, lift slowly up into the fan of light and much faster fall. A word cried aloud told him what he could not believe even as his numbed brain made sense, believed, and found the same word: crocodile.

Not one, however, nor a few, but scores of them were lumbering out of the mud, up the beach, and into the lines of overcrowded men. The only firing was spasmodic. Long gurglings came with insensate babble. Men ran and toppled as if over trip-wires. A leg spun up and stayed at a weird angle as if its owner were hand-standing. Then it vanished. A thump hit He-Setsu's boot, but as he recoiled he could see only the hillock and a receding tapered tail. He had not moved in a half minute, nor did he unroot himself as the moon came on strong. The beach writhed as the men ran into one another trying to get inland, only to run into another flock of men from the other side of the island, at this point only three hundred yards wide. The only way off the low promontory was to the right, from which men came running too. Indiscriminate shooting came from all quarters now, even from the higher land. Machine-gunners seemed to be firing into their own men. He-Setsu heard only faintly, his mind wounded. Already a pink-gray compost of dismembered soldiers hid the sand as the rioting crocodiles thrashed about with a hiss and ran, more of them than of men. He saw men actually scampering over low, corrugated backs, then felled like animals caught in foot-traps. He saw arms flung up in V's; a survivor diving into the shallows only to be raised up flailing like a bird; and, worst of all, red filaments of disemboweled men being dragged this way and that, like the strands of a dividing cell. At that point he wondered why he himself had not been attacked and, knowing only that he had not moved, stood on in aghast paralysis even as a new screaming began inland. The crocodiles had moved ahead, but others were coming from the sea to shuffle through the trail of carnage. Advancing on a broad front, he absently remarked. They cannot see me. I am alive. I am not hurt. I have not behaved like an officer.

2

A moment later he became infatuated with his immunity and knew he stood on a reef of fame, velvet-toed, iron-heeled, perdurably elect. An avatar, an idol, a force.

It was fully an hour before the uproar ended. He-Setsu hardly saw one hundred, two hundred, crocodiles pad like roaches back to the sea. Then a burst of gunfire raked the beach, fired by a demented survivor. A round grazed He-Setsu's skull, and he fell among the remnants of his men.

3

I am the biography of Lt. He-Setsu, but I am not his biographer; I am the re-entry, not its explainer. I am the fact, not its idea, and so cannot tell why he survived the crocodile attack, in which a couple of hundred slaughtered 1,160 of the 1,200 troops trapped on the island. History wanted him, no doubt, as did the reference books, and history curbs both minotaurs and crocodiles. After all, the random is forever with us: out of two thousand radium atoms, one dies each year, no more, no fewer. Yet why, since all two thousand are identical, do not all of them suffer the same fate at the same time? No one knows. Neither do I, who am the biography behaving at random like Nature.

There is more to come, too, of our Lt. He-Setsu. Left for dead by the remaining few, who survived because no second wave of crocodiles but a relief party from a boat came up the beach, he came to, unthinkingly waded through the maroon slop of the mud, and washed his wound. Then he stumbled inland, as high as he could go, settled behind a machine gun, and viewed the mosaic below of ballooning middles, jagged limbs, and black still heads. The crocodiles had killed way beyond their capacity to eat. Yet they had not returned to their leavings. And, as history knows, they never came back to that island, which they had never visited before. So far as is known.

After an hour's miserable thought, Lt. He-Setsu opened his shirt and began to knife exploratory lines across and down his stomach, just breaking the skin. Soon it resembled a close-up of wickerwork and he still had not made the plunge. If he fainted, he didn't remember the faint's onset. The blood congealed. His head hammered. Nothing broke the even spread of ocean. On he sat, an island upon an island of the dead, grimly reminded of white silk scarves which a Japanese girl would give her sweetheart to make him invulnerable in war. No such scarf had come his way.

On the one hand, he could sit where he was and solve all problems by starving to death. On the other hand, he could commit *seppuku* there and then. But why do either? Turn cannibal instead.

Out of the blue a salvo of shells straddled the island, all but one missing. Shaking dirt off himself, Lt. He-Setsu found he was unhurt. It occurred to him that, if only he found himself in a jungle and not on a bare finger of an island, he could remain there forever, living off the land. Torn between shame and the glory of being exempt, he fingered his sword and then chose: not honor, but deference to fate. Perhaps I am dead already, he mused, wincing at the cuts on his stomach. There is nothing else to do. This is my lot. I am home. Fate will tend me now.

But he was wrong. Only a day later, he was captured by U.S. Marines, mopping up, who found on a knoll only forty feet high a white-haired, blood-caked approximation to a man, impenetrably silent and rigid in a squat. They had to lift him up as he was. During interrogation he was unable to explain to the Nisei sergeant how he had survived; it was as if the interrogator were asking why men bore sperm and women eggs.

Perhaps, he told them all, destiny awaited him, years hence. A raised eyebrow was the only response he saw. His one prayer was never to meet the other survivors.

4

He never did. It is not known why. I am only his biography, not his exegete. What little help we have consists in his post-war audacity. Driven by some nagging sense of purpose, he took to studying mazes, not as decoration but as replicas of his own life situation. Not as puzzles but as cosmic emblems. For two years he designed and built some mazes in private or public gardens, often doing the digging and planting by himself. Thinking of the crocodiles, as he unrelentingly did, he worked fast. Next, however, he decided to do something serious and, in the dead of winter on Hokkaido, the northern island of Japan, initially with help from astounded peasants who had never been paid so much, built a life-or-death maze with enormous blocks of ice.

Alone, in his parka and airman boots, with a small fire, an ice-saw, and a big thermos of hot *sake*, he stood in the center of his finished maze and dropped the one and only plan into the flames. An hour and a quarter later he strode through the refreezing slush the fire had made and stamped out the embers. Then he drank all the *sake*, stripped off his parka and boots, and bearing the ice-saw before him looked for the way out. Lt. He-Setsu was repossessing his survival and, through it, his chance of death. It is not known what metaphysical yearnings occupied him during his last hours in the ice-warren, but his biography says he froze to death at the kneel, facing south. He no longer had the ice-saw. His stomach was bared and much scarred, as well as glued with recent blood.

No one has gone in; but, when the ice melts in a month or two, his corpse will fit into a legend everybody knows. And his name will come to life again.

17.
Sinbad's Head

*I*n every library there is a book that kills. Never iden-
tified, it is restored to its shelf after being found, innocuous,
among the clutter beside its victim's corpse. I know because
I have schooled myself to mark the signs, even in perfunctory
newspaper accounts, which, if one is lucky, mention the *Forever Amber* found on the bed of a mailman in Seattle or the
Gulliver's Travels in the backpack of a broker who fished in
waders off Padre Island, Texas.

Who is to know? No scalpel-sharp page-end slices the wrist.
No deadly gas emanates from within the volume's spine. No
radioactive spot disguised as a letter or a period hums into
the bloodstream. Yet the book kills with unique efficiency;
and some books, I believe it, have been around long enough
to become multiple murderers.

One such, part of whose career I now record, is an unlikely
tome entitled *Sinbad's Head*, published in New York by Maurer
in 1899. Its author, one Coburn Savage, with no other book
to his credit, lived the quiet life of a retired dentist in Seaport,
Maine, himself passing on in 1923. That his book is grisly
and brought grisly circumstances about, I admit, but there
is much more to this affair than mere subject matter. Indeed,
I judge Savage not in the least to blame for subsequent events.
Perhaps he died of pneumonia when he did for having penned
such a book, through some unspeakable feedback from his
creation into his mind. There is no knowing, but not one
copy of *Sinbad's Head* was found in his house or even a hol-
ograph in the attic. His publishers long ago melted away,
first absorbed by Macmillan early in the present century, and
then as it were regurgitated. Not even the name lasted. Of
the five vapid titles advertised in the endpapers, no copy has
come my way, although two repose in the British Museum.
Sinbad's Head is unique in several ways, as will soon be made
clear; but, foul as it is, it is only incidentally malefic, a piece
of some evil web which spans oceans and continents and the

very history of *homo sapiens* himself.

One sunny November day in 1958, I happened to return half a dozen miscellaneous volumes to the enormous library of the state university where I once taught bugle and trumpet and for fifteen years conducted the Blue Band. Wandering into the open stacks, I ended up on level three, drawn there, as so often to other levels and other stacks, by the random magnetism that has decided my reading for me over the past ten years. I believe to this day that a book calls out to us, summons us to its service, and repays the effort much more than books merely chosen. Attuned, you find books choosing you. (Try it.) The title in question, in shredded, hardly decipherable gilt on a black spine-panel, hit my eyes first as *Sin*, and then I saw *bad's Head*, concise enough as nonfiction titles go and evocative, to me, of exotic Arabian adventures in magical caves and on shipboard. I saw baggy pajamas, bright scimitars, a whole range of festive anachronisms into which strayed Aladdin's lamp and John the Baptist's severed head. My imagination is nothing if not lush.

Half a pound in weight, and faded from exposure to stack light rather than worn by use, *Sinbad's Head*, I found, was an account at second hand of how two surgeons removed a tumor from the brain of a Lebanese sailor fallen sick in London in 1885. At St. Vincent's Infirmary on Connaught Street. There is, was, no such institution on that street, and doubtless no such sailor or tumor existed. Yet, after only minutes, in my mind there was, and no wonder. I now reproduce, from *Sinbad's Head*, the passage I first read: "All his organs and functions were normal except that he, Sinbad, suffered from frequent violent paroxysmal attacks of lancinating pain in the head. There was complete paralysis of the left fingers, thumb, and hand. All the circumstances pointed to an encephalic growth on the right side." I gulped, twice.

"Neither bromide and iodide of potassium, twenty grains thrice daily, nor ice to the head, gave relief. Only hypodermic injections of morphia relieved the sailor's pain. So lines were drawn on his shaven head, and on November 26 a trephine one inch in diameter was applied and a circle of bone removed."

Almost too shocked to go farther, yet knowing I would, I then turned to the back of the book, discovering it had been charged out only twice. I, then, was the third to be fascinated by the callous jocularity of surgeons who ignored this poor creature's true name and dubbed him "Sinbad," perhaps blurring the horrors of their performance by making the victim generic. Had he been a Mexican, they would have called him Pancho, I suppose; if a strong man, Samson; although, if a Mexican strong man, I knew not what. Happily for the two doctors, his strain and calling matched an archetype and so made matters easier. Sinbad he was.

Yet who, I wondered, had preceded me at this feast of appetizing lies. I resolved to find out, such being my obsession with chance and the vagaries of taste. Cindy Lisle, a young circulation librarian of my acquaintance (of whose circulation a year previously I had had deeper knowledge), agreed to hunt the date down provided I once and for all ceased pestering her for encores, she being only thirty-eight. Off home I went, having secured the book on a four-week loan, and settled down on the smeared ottoman to read.

I quickly refound my place and continued. "A large Volkmann's spoon," I read, "was employed to scrape out the deeper parts of the growth until only healthy brain matter remained. No artery of any size spouted, but there was a general oozing, which accumulated rapidly as soon as the sponge was removed. The cavity thus left was about 1½ inches in depth and of a size into which a pigeon's egg would fit."

There followed some speculation about the wisdom of arresting hemorrhage by means of the galvano-cautery, which left behind it dangerous detritus. Savage, the ostensible dentist, questioned the advisability of introducing a drainage tube (as if a man accustomed to peering into mouths could say

Open Sesame to brains as well; as if tumor-removal were a mere extraction). On he went, fast antagonizing me with his knowing fibs. Enough to say that, during the entire two-hour operation, Sinbad took chloroform without a bad symptom. Subsequent examination revealed a tumor (a glioma) of walnut size, an amazing trophy to come out of the head of any human being at all. Alas, inflammation followed, and a month later Sinbad was dead of meningitis.

The reader may well marvel at my being able to stomach such a gruesome history at all. I suspected lies, of course, but couldn't be sure. Perhaps Savage had merely told the truth in the wrong terms, mistaking a street here, tilting an event there. At any rate, even with credulity strained, I could not deny myself the tale of what ensued (I sometimes wonder if we need the truth at all): an account of Sinbad's behavior shortly after death. It seems he began to talk volubly in English, carried on conversations with imaginary persons, and recited the most elaborate and yet lucid adventures. Hallucinations or no, what he said spellbound the surgeons; myself as well, aware as I was that Savage might simply have gone off his head.

As may I.

Should I go on? Dare I?

I have nothing to lose.

In his day, or maybe in a previous incarnation, Sinbad had been a professional storyteller, until a murder in a coffee house had made him flee, first to the Soko de Barra, a large bazaar of Tangier, a foul slope of viscous mud or powdery dust (depending on the weather), dotted with graves and decaying tombs, grimy booths, gargottes and tattered tents, a hive of camels and of men who squabbled over cattle for Gibraltar meat eaters. Here, in a broad waist belt into which his lower chiffons were tucked, and with a tom-tom shaped like an hourglass (on which he tapped with a stick to punctuate his narrative), he narrated, grimaced, and pantomimed his way through a hundred tales and more. A veritable Wonderland of cities and palaces of gold and silver, of priceless chargers and impossible cups, flowed from him, dazing and dazzling his hearers. Jinns and Jinniyahs, demons and fairies, wizards and sorcerers, lamias and cannibals, mermen and flying horses and reasoning elephants, all sprang from his lips. One of his stories, about himself, impressed his London doctors deeply, and I here recapitulate its elements, so that you can judge for yourselves the uncanny coincidences that came about.

One way of telling a story, he told them, was to remove the roof of a house so as to view the occupants as they cavorted. Yet the thought of it gave him inexplicable headaches (even then!). So, subject to increasing pain in the skull, Sinbad consulted various wizards, only the last of whom (of course) made sense of his condition. "Sinbad," crowed this charlatan, "thy brain is congested with a clot of blood which, swelling as if within a womb, will turn into a fetus. Thy head will distend until, at they term, thou wilt give birth, in a manner singularly befitting thee, to thy successor. This is when the roof of thy own head lifts up. Thy progeny will be the spawn of all the superfluous lies thou hast been accomplice to these thirty years."

Thus threatened with both an abnormal brainchild and a replacement in one, Sinbad thereupon took passage to Cairo to procure an abortion and desisted from his standard practice of lifting roofs.

An awful professional crisis followed.

No longer could he peer into bedchambers or eavesdrop. His tales became dull, speculative, in the end mere apologies for themselves: stories about stories being no longer possible owing to the incapacity, through pregnancy, of Sinbad himself. What a mess! At length, the only story remaining to him was his own. Lest he be stoned or impaled, he fled in disguise to sea as, first, a vendor of "blood, musk, and hashish" (such became his street cry), then as a common sailor with no wares at all save his muscles and his charm. And he never told a story again, his past a mere kenspeckle figment on his mental retina (until, that is, he babbled to the surgeons in London, telling them finally how the brain child miscarried in a half-hour nosebleed during a storm at sea).

Dazzled despite myself by Savage's shameless confection, I wondered even more at the identity of the book's two other borrowers. I telephoned Cindy Lisle, who dictated two names, two addresses, and then hung up. A long story can sometimes be short, and I give here only the bones, without apology.

The names were Ferrier and Woodsmoor, the former being the first to take out the book called *Sinbad's Head* and, as my researches also revealed, an amputee living leglessly not a mile away from me, in the Shenandoah Garden Apartments, on a war pension. A former Navy pilot, Major Ferrier had been obliged to parachute into the glacial waters of the Yellow Sea. Happily, it turned out, a rescue helicopter was on its way to him within ten minutes in response to his Mayday call. His story, I discovered, was well known in this neighborhood, in certain circles at any rate. Unhappily, the paramedic who leapt into the sea rescued and sent up by winch Major Ferrier's downed opponent, a North Korean of course, and this altruistic bungler's name was Woodsmoor. In the end, the helicopter found and rescued Ferrier too, but not before his legs were numbed beyond redemption. For this, once he learned the full truth, he never forgave Woodsmoor and kept track of him ever afterward, finally after years of slow-baked animus running down his man and choosing his moment.

I surmise, of course. Why else should Woodsmoor, a well-established male attendant at an Ohio nursing home, drive three hundred miles to a small town in the East, check in for two nights at a Sheraton motel, and after a good night's sleep check out *Sinbad's Head* at the campus library? I imagine the plea from Ferrier, craving talk about the old days, after which Woodsmoor would agree to fetch the book for the legless victim of his onetime incompetence. What interests me above all is that Ferrier survived his first borrowing of the book, when he took it out in his own name (or had it taken out for him). Maybe that proxy died soon after, whereas Ferrier, perhaps for having been dead technically or given up for lost, and then amputated, no longer counted among the living. Who knows? There will always be mysteries.

No one seems to know much beyond Woodsmoor's body being found on his motel bed next morning, struck down by an infarction, with *Sinbad's Head* nearby. Only I link the two men lethally. I suspect Ferrier, of course, but what can I prove? I cannot, yet, fathom why Woodsmoor took out the book in his own name (I know visitors can) and ended up keeping it instead of getting it to Ferrier. I marvel at my being the only one to detect the book's charge-sheet as linking the legless Ferrier with his inadvertent maimer Woodsmoor.

Clearly, I should keep my own counsel, unless I wish to be thought mad. Daily I ponder patterns in time, the ways in which a convoluted tale of a tumor, removed in London from a no doubt fictitious Arabian, becomes an instrument of death for an amputee in the habit of having books fetched for him. It is as if he had requisitioned a guillotine. The book I keep on renewing; no one requests it, it is never called in. So I am almost certainly weaving myself into the fabric of past and present disaster. Yet it would matter little if the police should investigate the book's borrowing history. I might even pluck up the courage to confront Ferrier himself; but, if so, my visit will have to be soon.

For several weeks, especially after reading the book, I have been experiencing just such lancinating head pains as it describes. My own eyes and tongue, like Sinbad's, deviate leftward in conjugate error. A faint paralysis grows daily worse. I am aware of babbling irresponsibly to myself, even by phone to Cindy Lisle, who hangs up as always, although she has not yet reported me. Jinns and goblins, eunuchs and knights, rustling pavilions and talking fishes, greet me nightly from my pillow, sometimes even at breakfast. There cannot be long to go; so, within the next few days, I will tear out of the book the pages describing Sinbad's moribund outbursts and enclose them, as the nub of trouble, in a prestamped envelope addressed to Ferrier, and entrusted to my attorney for postmortem mailing. The mutiliated book, microcosm of me, as of us all, can go back to the library and will no doubt be withdrawn from circulation, yet how replaced? As if it were a soul. Alongside the last date stamp will appear my farewell: *This book has killed me.* Let who wishes ponder *Sinbad's Head* in his own way, and, if he dares to, take it out. Oh, spittle of Allah, it is killing me even now. I see, I know; I see much farther, I know more, I. . . .

I refashion my beginning. The books that kill are not in libraries only, but everywhere; good, unsuicidal folk buy them, prize them, make of them gifts and high-priced rarities. Hence so many deaths daily, all caused by books, instant or delayed. One widely read book might kill thousands if only they'll read it; unread, however, it has no lethal clout at all.

Or so I thought as I dwindled into merely spasmic flesh, host to the gorged walnut in my head. Why, then, I wondered, do the illiterate die, who know nothing of books. Or primitives. Pre-Caxton humans. Pre-papyrus brothers. Their pre-Mosaic-tablet forbears. Before caves had walls. The answer is that not the book but the story kills. That must be it. Certain *stories* are fatal in the long or the short run, and those are stories in which the teller shows awareness of having to come to an end, whereas the story without end, ah yes!, the story whose teller shows no self-awareness at all, and tells on and on, beyond his own body's end and the end of humankind, rejoicing without guile in the holy immortality of the imagination, sap of the cosmos, ah yes! That one unwritten unwritable eggs us on, eggs even me, will save us all and Sinbad too. I *will not* die. What swells in my head, sucks me white, and twists me gimpy is nothing malignant but the nucleus of that which, once begun, has no ending.

So I rebegin anew, as enclosed in words as a Sinbad, writing the words "Every library," but destined never again to reach this penultimate point. I am the heir of Sinbad's head, which libraries cannot contain and tumors cannot kill.

18.
The Universe,
and Other Fictions

*I*t sits now, as for the past 5,050 days, in their Museum of Runes, on a black electronically protected plinth in the Coalsack Room, alongside it the cassette holding the tape of what came off it when it was first played. An ordinary-looking LP, but with no logo on the white disc at its center, it spun once to awful effect, yielding almost an hour of unprecedented talk, and then lapsing silent, self-erased into a blank. Again and again they set it on turntables, but all they heard was the amplified scrape of the stylus. Yet to them it remains a compelling relic, a Stonehenge of the ear, almost as baffling as the tape of its contents, the one rotary, the other linear. Not a household, by now, that doesn't have its copy of the tape, merchandized cheap by Amalgamated World Churches under the title of The Recording of April 1, 19 etc. Its origin most have forgotten (who having manna credits heaven?), but I remember only too well how it arrived in the morning mail of the Secretary General of Nations United, though why he resigned only months later remains unclear.

At any rate, to make a fabula rasa of all this, I smile tolerantly at my own interfering nature, then begin the umpteenth run-through of my one and only fiction, sometimes hearing the flip-side first, so as not to be biased. But not today. Side One, as always, comes through loud and clear, even a mite bullhorn in its direct accost.

Side 1.

"Steady now. I am the universe, come before you as a local character, talking your slang, wearing a patchwork suit of green fields and red Virginia earth, the whole held together by a pretty stitching of fences and low shrubs, with conch shells for toenails, moss for body hair, limestone in my knee-cap and tinkling fresh-water springs in either tear duct. A festive variety of silverfish, rabbits, herons, lions, and bison overruns my frame. I'd like to be friendly, in some impossibly selfless way. And, if I can't rise to positive show, limiting myself to boons terrestrial, I'd at least like to seem other than the Enemy: merchant of virus and bacterium, wholesale dealer in murrain, anthrax, glaucoma, cancer, dementia, the rest. I'd like to come on strong as friend to man. With backslap. Handshake. Nose-rub. A shoulder-to-shoulder stance against some common enemy we won't even name.

"Alas, these are pipe dreams all. I can't even come on amiably strong as the mediocre star of your local system, or as one of the biceped arms of your Milky Way. I'm bound, it seems, through some democratic quirk in the manifold, to speak always as the Many, whose One I remain. There is no opting for this or that partial voice, this or that life form, intelligent or otherwise; or even, in its death pangs, aphid, white dwarf, or quasar. Obligated to the whole, I can only moan round you with many voices, in flawless harmony, if you can stomach the term; and, no matter how hard I try to come down to Earth and level with you, I end up bringing the All with me. Too big for my own good. In other words, my friends, I am not allowed impromptu synecdoches, as when you yourselves manage to say *head* for *cattle*, or *the law* for *a policeman*: the part for the whole, the whole for a part. Indeed, of all the parts I would wholly play, all are taboo, which is why, if you forgive the seeming plagiarism, I ultimately have to commit fiction, thus helping myself to a human solace, stealing a human show. Not that I'd ask very much; I'd dearly like to come before you, as I said, in arable motley, and say: *Here is my calling card, read it.* Or: *May I offer you a light?* Or: *If you need the price of a sandwich* . . . But it would turn out wrong. My card would incinerate or liquefy your eyeballs. The light I proffered would blister your milky-blue planet. The money I forked out would have to be repaid in firebolts. Why, the kiss of life from me would strike you dead, as it eventually does anyway. My grin cooks. My dreams rend. My good will freezes.

"Yet, fair's fair. I'm known as a steady fellow, stable and even-tempered, forever in the middle of the road, having neither beginning nor end. I no more have family tree than I have eschatology. So you can perhaps see why, in my milder moments, I long to spend just a day as a spider, an elk, a whale, or even (shifting into terms you cannot know) one of the Cybionts who inhabit Crinkniz, planet in a galaxy you will never find. Out of the question: the part of me that isn't involved in the fiction knows it isn't, and thus gives the lie to the whole endeavor.

"Heavens, I'd love to get away from things. I weary of being thought such a decent, stable, all-round good egg, as the idiom has it. The provider. The go-between. The Universe voted most likely to succeed. On the small scale, I'd love to graduate *cum laude* (I wouldn't care who did the praising either) from almost anywhere. Or invest my all in a little red-fanged compact car that never went faster than sixty or seventy, or a hundred. Say a good round hundred and fifty miles per hour. Well, perhaps three or four hundred. If not that, then publish a book, preferably pornographic enough to cause a scandal, make me an object of notoriety. Or, failing that, fondle a girl in a summerhouse while the rain of any season tap-danced on the roof. Sentimental? Ah me, yes. But that is the side of me you'd prefer, compared to another that seems, year after year, under the influence of some malefic force—a double, an alias, a competitor who has resorted to voodoo—which gets me itching to sally out of character. Kick over the traces, see. Kick the traces out of sight. Kick the kishkes out of every second galaxy. Play hell with all things bright and beautiful and then, quite curtly, just kick off.

"You won't credit it, but in the worst of those bad moods, good guy I swing through the gamut of exotic abominations. Like these:

"Bash a ball into someone's face.

"Chop wood till it bleeds.

"Smoke myself to death.

"Rape anacondas, filthily wriggling.

"Stomp on fledglings.

"Hunt lion with axe and laser gun.

"Go cannibal in the Alps, venting a grease-thick yodel.

"Scream for an eon.

"But no. Stranded between alpha and omega (as at least one cosmic formula has it), my flesh is grass, but is so much else as well. I dream it all, take it out in little shrugs. I am especially deficient in credulity, which makes all my fictions return to the original bind. My *Thousand and One Nights*, for example, palls in the context of all the unincluded nights. Thank your lucky stars you do not know too much, as I, losing heart's desire in surfeit. Remember me as the pageant of a will, with my dreams haunted by some rival louder and lustier than I; yet obliged to soldier on, brain-sick with the golden mean, the middle road, the pathic splendor of keeping calm.

"Cheerio. Pity me, but not too much. Let this universe, this Verse, built on the equivalent of a hill overlooking lakes and rich valleys, surrounded by woods and farms, instill in its inhabitants more than an appreciation of the power of flinty intelligence to guess, to plumb, to fathom. I mean, rather, through the pressure of beauty's presence, to impart a deep sense of the privilege that living is, altogether, as one. Do not envy. By no means copy anything I do. Be content. Eye your only moon. Bow to the stars. You die; I do not. You were all born, I not. I renew and renew, intransitively; but I do not renew you. You are the Many, I the One. Get set. Steady. Go. There, I got it out again, without running amok."

Side 2.

"Bang-bang, and I was born. In my beginning, I was all gas and no intentions. I didn't even hurt. After five minutes, I cooled down, I lost interest in the passing of the time, and, if I feel any nostalgia now, it's for the good old days of the first minutes, when radiant energy prevailed and I was a billion degrees hot. Like a baby born in the tropics. It was humbling to have fallen to only a quarter of that after half an hour, oh yes, and then a mere six thousand after two hundred thousand years, and then a hundred degrees below the freezing point of water on my two-hundred-fifty-millionth birthday. You can see I've got my biography off by heart.

"Hail, holy hydrogen, I thought. That was all I *said* for millions of years, in fact, long before the gossip began and self-styled pundits devised insolent assignments for helpless students, such as: 'Define the word *universe*. Give two examples.' I have a sense of humor, of course, it's only natural. Over so long a period, it's bound to come. But surely there are limits.

"As I was saying, I had no idea what to expect before the beginning, so to speak. Perhaps it really went floof, woosh, bang. Or bang, woosh, floof. Or even woosh, floof, bang. You know how permutations go. The problem was that there was no order for events to come in. Just a lot of heavy breathing at the assembly line. Hey, hee, high, ho, hue. Hey, hee, hy-drogen, in fact. *Ad nauseam*, with the big blank Sunday holiday looming, everything closed down, and everyone hanging around with nowhere to go.

"Do you wonder, then, that I'm thought capricious, testy, forever going off half-cocked? The most upsetting thought of all was that of there being a time, a space, when I wasn't there. It was only much later, on my time scale at any rate, that I got to look at the eyewitness accounts, especially the Mosaic verse that included the most famous subjunctive of all time: *Let there be light*. I gasped: H—, H—, H—, H . . . And light there was, unbroken, out of nowhere. I could see my breath for the first time, not clouding a window, of course, or smoking horn-shaped in the November chill. (Or was it December?) Nothing so modern. And I said to myself: 'How did Moses know?' How did he (presuming he was not a committee) know that the word *light* existed before light itself did? Who was here, eavesdropping on that preposterous fit of the godly get-up-and-go? Had a bribe changed hands, I wondered. Had Moses agreed not to hide the light under a bush in exchange for the divine low-down? I even got to the point of thinking that I generated light myself, as one might fling off a little sweat while stretching on a hot day, and someone else took all the crdit. No, I reassured myself, all that stuff took place before anything was. It was unverifiable. A rumor. A positive opinion in the absence of evidence. Myth reposes. Hypothesis proposes. Fiction poses. H—m, I told myself: *Moses poses*. A liar. And that was that.

"A long time after the light, it was intimated to me (or I imagined) that, among billions of life forms, one in particular would groom that Mosaic guess into theology and holy texts, chanting and droning its corollaries. All that plain-chant fuss about a bit of algebra. I might even have felt resentful except that, in my impulsively minifying way, I scaled down planet Earth's history to one of its vaunted calendar years, so that Earth's origin dated from January 1st, and Man showed up at 11:50 p.m. on December 31st, not so much Johnny Come Lately as a Johnny Hardly Come At All, with all recorded terrestrial history falling into the final forty seconds of the year. Paltry. Petty. Picayune. At least, that's how it seemed to one, the only Uni, who is around twelve billion years or more old. My origins were cloudy; my future is nebulous beyond the quality of known clouds; but my present is as near perpetual as makes no difference. I am entitled to be censorious of planetary upstarts who underrate my scope, slander my birth, guess at my demise. Pah! Bad-tempered I might have become with advancing years, but I still call a spade a spade.

"There have been other bad-mouthings as well. To all suggestions that I am finite, I just go on being myself, expanding at will. My galaxies are as uniformly spread out as the flocks in a new pillow of the old-fashioned kind. My curvaceousness is negative, which means my triangles add up to less than one hundred and eighty degrees. Nor do I respond well to suggestions that I pulse, or vacillate, wax and shrink nonstop, am volatile. No, from an infinitely thin state an eternity ago I shrank until I reached maximum density, from which I rebounded never to look back.

"See how much information I have? Uncanny, isn't it?

"Note the civility of my tone as well, my courtesy in choosing your language, my helpfulness in using your own units of measurement. Have your fellow beings treated you half as well? Will they ever? Not that I mean to talk down, but you might consider a few things more. You have nowhere else to go. You have no satisfactory knowledge of me. I have never yet chosen to be jailed in your jargon. Whatever you do affects me, but I am too big to mind. All that happens *to* you happens *in* me. I am an envelope, a holder, a hugger, a clasper, a kisser. I am the figure for which there is no ground. When I breathe, I exhale more than I took in. Listen. I—n. O—u—t. I am the monopolist of the going-awayness of everything. I do not need alpha or omega, infinity or zero. *I am.* And I act before I think, like a camel dropping dung in a Cairo gutter, or ancient beasts coupling on the run. When I move, I move. When I mate, I—well, I do not mate. I am the class of all classes that are not members of themselves.

"I am foamy. I froth.

"I curve around everything.

"I am paraplegia to the nth.

"I detest all fishers of men.

"I kick.

"I chop.

"I smoke.

"I cannot read.

"I fry fish all the time.

"I midnight-snack.

"I balance.

"I communicate.

"I climb high.

"I aim higher.

"I dunk my bread.

"I am incurably dry-eyed. I will not tell how the ship got into the bottle, nucleus into cell. I gasp on. Hear me now: the emphysema of osmosis. I huff and I puff and blow down the housing of mankind.

"Ha. Ha-ha. A-hem. And on we go, breathless. As a buffalo I say thwunk. As a mamba I say hnip-hnip. As a trout I say thwoo. As a tufted titmouse I say a lively whistled peter-peter-peter, or a scolding nasal ya-ya-ya. Of course I play favorites. All the time. Look in your hospitals. And, any century, any eon, any epoch, I can be found up to my old solitary games, among a gam of whales, a drift of hogs, a dule of doves, chanting *Menschentotenlieder* that go: 'O be a fine girl, kiss me now,' a little stellar spectrum snatch, or 'Bagdei,' catch that reminds me of the star order in Cassiopeia. Why not come up and see me sometime? We have a date. Up is down. Out is in. Past is before. Now is then. Why not reinvest your all in me? You see the problem: with each human brain worth only about ten watts' electrical power, just think how many billions of heads, I mean brains, to get back to my original power, as it was in the first thirty seconds of life. To which state I intend returning, with you as grist for my mill, manure to my mind. How about it then? I'll make you one with Nature, as the poets used to say in old, heart-fondling romantic elegies for drowned friends.

"There! Caught myself at it again. Talking to oneself is lonelier than self-abuse. Men can't hear. God isn't. There is only lonely I, twitchy, moody, flashy victim of my birth, jerked into being like I don't know what. Enough. I go. Don't accept any effigies. Breathe deep. Eat your hearts out, as I mine. Remember this: truth is more likely to be a midwife's thump on your buttocks than it is an infolded rose. H—, alo-H-a."

It still sits where I said it sat, as for the past 5,050 days, the black platter I wiped clean, while humans of all sorts and conditions play and replay the two-track runic tape. Let them. Let them be. Let there—no, that's already written. Let there be something else, then, even if only a novelty to make them rearrange the contents of the Coalsack Room. A platter with a third side, a fourth, a fifth, like an ebony thunderbolt careening through a tube made of time. No doubt of it, I'll think of something soon. All week I shovel atoms, toil in the abyss of the cosmic hold; but, Sunday, absolute fiction be praised, I invent, and hydrogen's the prose.